"What makes you think I'd settle for friend-ship?" Jason asked.

Maggie saw the challenge in his eyes and suspected Jason wasn't used to having some-one else make the rules. But she couldn't let herself be taken in by charm and good looks. With five children to care for, she couldn't lose her head over a confirmed bachelor.

"Friendship is all I have to offer at this time," she said firmly.

"At this time?" he asked.

"Well, if I *do* decide to get serious with a man, it will be with someone older, more mature. I'm not looking to be swept off my feet. At my age, I'm more interested in security," Maggie said.

He laughed. "Thirty-three? Maggie, darlin', I think you *do* want to be swept off your feet." She started to object, and he put his finger to her lips. "You're just too scared and stubborn to admit it. But I know what you want. It's written all over your pretty face. I see it every time I look into those gorgeous green eyes." He traced her mouth with his finger. "When a man makes love to you, you want the earth to move. . . ."

WHAT ARE *LOVESWEPT* ROMANCES?

They are stories of true romance and touching emotion. We believe those two very important ingredients are constants in our highly sensual and very believable stories in the *LOVESWEPT* line. Our goal is to give you, the reader, stories of consistently high quality that may sometimes make you laugh, sometimes make you cry, but are always fresh and creative and contain many delightful surprises within their pages.

Most romance fans read an enormous number of books. Those they truly love, they keep. Others may be traded with friends and soon forgotten. We hope that each *LOVESWEPT* romance will be a treasure—a "keeper." We will always try to publish

LOVE STORIES YOU'LL NEVER FORGET
BY AUTHORS YOU'LL ALWAYS REMEMBER

The Editors

Charlotte Hughes

The Incredible Hunk

BANTAM BOOKS
NEW YORK · TORONTO · LONDON · SYDNEY · AUCKLAND

THE INCREDIBLE HUNK
A Bantam Book / February 1993

If you would be interested in receiving protective vinyl
covers for your Loveswept books, please write to this address
for information:

Loveswept
Bantam Books
P.O. Box 985
Hicksville, NY 11802

ISBN 0-553-44363-1

Published simultaneously in the United States and Canada

Bantam Books are published by Bantam Books, a division of
Bantam Doubleday Dell Publishing Group, Inc. Its trademark,
consisting of the words "Bantam Books" and the portrayal of
a rooster, is Registered in U.S. Patent and Trademark Office
and in other countries. Marca Registrada. Bantam Books, 666
Fifth Avenue, New York, New York 10103.

PRINTED IN THE UNITED STATES OF AMERICA
OPM   0 9 8 7 6 5 4 3 2 1

O: *Thanks for the idea*

One

"He's gorgeous, isn't he?"

Maggie Farnsworth swept her copper-colored hair from her forehead and took a long look at Crescent City's new soccer coach. Standing on the field amid an ocean of freckle-faced, snaggle-toothed eight- and nine-year-olds, the man struck an imposing figure with his wide shoulders, blond hair, and tempting backside. Buns to die for, Maggie thought. "You're right, he *is* a hunk." In fact, he was the best-looking thing she'd ever laid eyes on—Kevin Costner included. He moved with an easy grace despite his powerful, well-muscled body. "What do you know about him?" she asked her friend, studying him in a way that was totally uncharacteristic of her.

Cynthia Lansing leaned closer. Divorced only half as long as Maggie, she had the stats on every healthy, unattached male between the ages of twenty-five and fifty within a forty-mile radius of Crescent City, Georgia.

"Jason Profitt," she replied. "Thirty years old, never been married, engineer." She ticked off his qualifications with the same enthusiasm one might list the ingredients of a much-loved candy recipe.

Maggie arched one reddish-brown brow. "Never been married?"

"That's what I hear. He's from West Palm Beach, Florida. That's where all the money is, you know. Why, you interested?"

Maggie chuckled. "Me, interested in a *man*? Get real, Cynthia. Besides, don't you think he's a little young for me?"

"Three years? That's nothing. Anyway, you don't look thirty-three, what with those freckles and that turned-up nose." Cynthia grinned as she said it. Anybody who knew Maggie Farnsworth knew she hated her freckles. She had tried bleaching them out with lemon juice and anything else folks suggested, and as a teenager she'd swallowed everything from raw egg to hot beer in hopes of ridding herself of them. Nothing had worked. "Why don't you introduce yourself to him after the game?" Cynthia said after a moment.

Maggie's lips thinned into a grim line. "Yeah, right."

"Now, that's no way to talk. Who knows, the two of you might hit it off?"

It was a tempting thought, the kind fairy tales were made of. Maggie wished she still believed in dreams and fairy tales. "Until he found out *certain things*," she said, sighing wistfully. "Then he'd tuck his tail and run."

"Don't tell him," Cynthia said. At the look Maggie shot her, she went on. "What I mean is, you don't have to blurt it out. Get to know him first."

"He's probably heard already. It's probably been engraved on the wall of the men's room at the Chevron station." She offered her friend a rueful smile. "Besides, why do I need a man? Isn't my life complicated enough?"

Cynthia clucked her tongue. "I don't understand you, Maggie. Here you are, always complaining how you don't have a life. How do you ever plan to get one, if you don't make an effort?"

Maggie was only half listening. Her gaze was riveted to the big man as he pulled the group of boys aside, going down on his haunches so that he was at eye level with them when he spoke. The boys seemed to cling to his every word. He was much too good-looking to be spending a Friday night with the peewee soccer team, she thought.

"He seems to get along well with the kids," Maggie whispered, although she suspected after a while he would lose interest in her son. Davey was smaller and quieter than most boys his age. As a result, he was often overlooked, lost in the crowd. Of course, he pretended it didn't matter, just as he pretended he didn't mind the fact that his father didn't have time for him. But Maggie knew better. She saw the evidence each time Davey carried his wet bed sheets to the washer and every time he chose to sit in his room and work puzzles instead of playing with the neighborhood children. For that she resented her ex-husband. Even when he *could* make time for his visits, Bob Farnsworth preferred his daughters to his son. Which was why Maggie had decided to sign the boy up for soccer and take him herself.

"He has to like children," Cynthia replied after a minute, "or he wouldn't be coaching."

The game started, and Maggie tried to concentrate on the boys instead of on their coach. It bothered her that she kept searching him out. She called out a word of encouragement to Davey, but it didn't help. He was slow and couldn't keep up with the other boys as they raced up and down the field. She could already see the lines of frustration on his face. Later he would sit in his room and brood about it. Maggie wanted to run out onto the field and take him in her arms. He would have been mortified, of course, so she didn't. Still, she was touched to the core when Jason Profitt hurried over to the boy, ruffled his red hair, and said something that brought a fleeting smile to his face.

"Well, we lost," Cynthia said once the game was over. "Coach Profitt certainly has his work cut out for him."

"Give him time," Maggie said. "Besides, this is only their second practice game." Maggie had missed the first practice two days earlier when she'd had to work late. Her boss was notorious for asking her to work overtime at the last minute. She didn't dare complain, though. Bob Farnsworth was about as dependable with his child support payments as he was with visitation. Luckily, Cynthia's daughter was on the same soccer team as Davey, so it hadn't been a problem for her to take him. But Maggie had suffered an enormous amount of guilt over it. Davey needed her, and she'd let him down. She was tired of apologizing to the boy.

Maggie chatted with her friend another few minutes while waiting for the bleachers to clear. Cynthia's daughter, Abby, joined them once they'd climbed down, complaining how rotten the team was. While Cynthia tried to offer some words of encouragement to the girl, Maggie scanned the crowd for her son. She found him and Jason standing in the middle of the field, talking. Her heart sank. Was his coach scolding him for how poorly he'd played? she wondered. Perhaps Jason was trying to convince the boy to try again next year, when he'd be taller and faster. She knew Davey would take it hard. Even so, she would prefer he be off the team than on the bench all season.

"I hope Mr. Profitt will give Davey a chance," she whispered to Cynthia as they strode closer, then waited at a respectful distance so coach and player could finish their conversation. Maggie knew how important this was for her son. If only he could excel at one thing! He needed something to boost his self-confidence. "I know he isn't very good right now, but he'll do better once he gets the hang of it."

"He and Abby can practice together," Cynthia said.

Maggie nodded, darting a look at her son and his coach every now and then. Finally, the man patted the boy on the shoulder, and they started walking toward the bleachers. "Oh, Lord, he's coming this way," she whispered, wringing her hands. "That can mean only one thing. Davey's off the team."

"Stop being so pessimistic," Cynthia told her. "It doesn't always have to be bad news. And smile."

It would have been easier to smile, Maggie told herself, if she hadn't dressed in her grungiest cutoffs and sneakers. But it was too late to worry about that. The next thing she knew, the coach was standing right in front of her.

"Mrs. Farnsworth?"

Maggie's mouth went dry. His hair was the color of ripened wheat, framing a tanned face that suggested he spent a lot of time outdoors. "Yes, I'm Maggie Farnsworth," she all but sputtered as a hot blush crept up her neck and stained her cheeks. He was even taller than she'd first thought, more powerfully built. He looked tough and lean and sinewy without compromising his boyish good looks.

"Jason Profitt." He extended his hand.

The hand that gripped hers was warm and strong, slightly rough, and for a moment Maggie simply enjoyed his touch, the feeling of protectiveness it imbued. She gazed up at the man and found herself looking into the most gorgeous blue eyes she'd ever seen.

"Nice to meet you, Mr. Profitt," she said, trying to make her voice sound natural despite the feeling of breathlessness that had stolen over her the minute he'd touched her. For a moment she merely stared at him. Cynthia nudged her. She jumped, then reluctantly pulled her hand free. "Oh, and this is my friend, Cynthia Lansing."

Jason shook hands with Cynthia before giving Maggie his undivided attention. "Listen, your son is going to need a little practice. I was wondering if you or your husband could work with him in your spare time."

Practice? Maggie felt herself nod. So her son wasn't being kicked off the team after all. She was giddy with relief.

"My dad doesn't live with us," Davey blurted out, surprising them both.

Jason glanced from Maggie to the boy and back again. He had clear, observant eyes. "Oh." The look on his face told Maggie he felt like a jerk for bringing it up.

"We're divorced," she told him, offering him a smile that was both understanding and forgiving. "But I can practice with Davey."

Jason nodded and smiled down at the boy. "I think Davey would make an excellent goalie," he said. "But I expect him to work at it."

Maggie didn't have any trouble reading between

the lines. A goalie? But of course. A goalie wouldn't have to keep up with the bigger, stronger boys. She wanted to hug Jason Profitt for suggesting it.

Maggie offered her son an enthusiastic smile. "Would you like to be the goalie?" she asked, hoping to impart some of that same enthusiasm to her son and take the look of uncertainty from his eyes. As she waited for Davey's response, she was uncomfortably aware of Jason. His gray short-sleeve sweatshirt was slightly damp around his neck and under his arms. His upper lip was beaded with sweat as well, and the hair on his forearms glistened. How very male he was, how virile, she thought. And she was staring at him for all she was worth! She pried her gaze loose.

Davey shrugged. "I probably won't be any good at it."

Jason put a big hand on the boy's shoulder and squeezed it reassuringly. Once again Maggie felt drawn to the man because of the simple display of affection toward her son. "Of course you will," he told the boy. "And if you'll come twenty minutes early next week, I'll practice with you before the others arrive." He looked the youngster right in the eye. "You know, Davey, the goalie is one of the most important players on the team. You'll have to work hard if you expect to be good at it. I guess it's up to you, though, whether or not you want to play that position."

"I do, Coach," the boy said earnestly.

"Great." He smiled, and the warmth of his expression echoed in his voice. "I'll expect you early next week."

It was all Maggie could do to keep from throwing her arms around the man's neck. Someone was finally taking an interest in her son. She beamed at him. "Thank you, Mr. Profitt," she said, inspired by the optimism he had for Davey. "We'll be here." She raised her eyes to his once more, and their gazes locked. She felt giddy and out of breath, as though she'd just run the entire length of the soccer field. She was simply happy for her son, she told herself. So why was she so reluctant to walk away from this blond giant, she thought, noting the parking lot was fast emptying, everyone obviously in a hurry to get home. "Well, we have to go now, Davey," she said, coming down from her momentary high to that place of normalcy and responsibility, where common sense reigned. She had absolutely no business looking at her son's coach that way. No business whatsoever. She smiled at the man once more, but this time her smile was tight and composed. For a moment there she had lost touch with reality, reading more into his looks and smiles than he'd obviously meant. "Thanks again," she said, all her defenses back in place as she strode away purposefully. Jason nodded and returned to the field for his gear.

"See, that wasn't so hard, now, was it?" Cynthia whispered. "What do you think of him?"

Maggie jumped when she realized she had forgotten Cynthia altogether. Trying to gather her wits, she watched as her son and Abby raced ahead. "He's gorgeous, of course, but definitely not my type." She paused. That didn't mean she wasn't grateful for the chance he was giving her son, though, she told herself.

"Exactly what *is* your type?"

They'd had this conversation before, Maggie knew, but it seemed she was forever reminding her friend. "Someone older. More mature. A man who isn't afraid of responsibility." She chuckled. "A *lot* of responsibility." She checked her wristwatch as they neared their cars. "I'd better hurry home," she said, "in case Bob decides to bring the girls back early." Cynthia followed and waited until Maggie had climbed behind the wheel of her station wagon.

"I noticed he was looking at your legs, Mag," she said with a grin.

Davey looked up for the first time. "Who was looking at Mom's legs?"

Maggie blushed. "Don't listen to Cynthia, honey," she told her son. "I think she got hit in the head with a stray soccer ball tonight." She slipped her key into the ignition and gave Cynthia a rueful smile. "If he *was* staring, it can only mean he's heard about me, and he was looking for stretch marks." She turned the key in the ignition.

Nothing happened.

"Oh, no!"

Cynthia frowned. "Don't tell me it's your battery again."

"Okay, I won't tell you." Maggie leaned her head against the steering wheel. "Do you know anything about batteries?"

Cynthia shook her head. "Honey, I wouldn't recognize a battery in a lineup."

"Having trouble, ladies?" a masculine voice asked, startling them both.

Maggie glanced up. Jason Profitt was standing a short distance away. "Oh, Mr. Profitt." She laughed self-consciously. "It's my battery. It always does this. I should be able to get it started in a minute."

Cynthia regarded the man. "You wouldn't happen to have a set of battery cables with you?"

"As a matter of fact, I do." He looked at Maggie. "I can jump-start you, if you like."

The way her heart fluttered in her chest, Maggie was tempted to tell him he already *had* her motor running on high. She blushed, and she could feel the heat clear to the ends of her fingertips. The only explanation she could think of for her body's strange behavior was that she was going through an early menopause. "Oh, I hate to put you to the trouble," she heard herself say.

"No trouble," he assured her.

"Great," Cynthia said. "Look, I was supposed to be somewhere ten minutes ago," she told Jason, "but I don't want to leave Maggie alone. Would you see that she gets out of here okay?"

When Maggie started to protest, Jason interrupted. "I don't mind. Do you have a hood release on this thing?" He was already moving to the front of the car.

"Thanks a lot, Cynthia," Maggie hissed to her friend as soon as Jason was out of earshot. "I thought you said you were going home to wash your hair. Don't leave me!"

"Stop acting like a ninny. It's not like you've never been around a man before." She chuckled. "Your reputation speaks for itself."

"That isn't funny, and you know it." Maggie watched Jason lift her hood, then make his way to his own car. A sports car. She should have known. Bachelors didn't drive station wagons. The last thing they wanted to be bothered with was children and grocery sacks. He climbed in and cranked the engine.

Cynthia leaned closer to the window of Maggie's car. "Now, when he gets your car started, be sure to thank him nicely and offer to buy him a cup of coffee sometime. But don't start giving him a bunch of *free information* about yourself, if you know what I mean. And stop frowning. He's simply jump-starting your car, not performing a root canal on you."

"I'm going to get you for this," Maggie said tightly, but Cynthia was already out of earshot, prodding her daughter toward their own car.

Maggie watched Jason pull his car right up to hers and climb out. He opened his trunk and produced a set of battery cables.

"I want to help Mr. Profitt," Davey said, opening his door and climbing out before Maggie could object. Besides, it was probably good for him, she thought, since the boy didn't spend much time in the company of men. She was more than a little pleased when Jason allowed Davey to assist him in putting the cables into place.

"Okay, go ahead and start it," Jason called out.

With trembling fingers Maggie turned the key in the ignition, and her engine came to life. Jason immediately detached the cables. "That ought to get you where you're going," he said once he'd closed the hood. "But I wouldn't turn off your motor in the meantime." He came closer to the window. "Frankly, I think you're going to need a new battery."

Maggie found it difficult to concentrate on the conversation when all she wanted to do was gaze into those blue eyes. "The one I have is still under warranty," she said, "but the guy at the automotive shop refuses to give me a new one. He put my battery on a charger last time and said that would fix it, but it didn't." Even as the words came out she couldn't help but wonder why she was telling him her troubles.

"Where'd you buy it?"

"A place called Friend's Automotive, owned and operated by Billy-Bob Friend. Only he's about as friendly as a rattlesnake." She reached into the glove compartment. "I even have a warranty, but he wouldn't honor it." She handed the paper to him.

Jason skimmed the document and saw that it was in order. "I know the guy. He and I butted heads a couple of weeks ago over a set of tires he sold me when I first moved here. You really should make him do something about it," he said. "Don't let the guy intimidate you just because you're a woman."

Maggie considered it. How refreshing it was to hear such a comment from a man. "You know, you're absolutely right. I'm going over there right now and demand a new battery."

Jason grinned. "Atta girl. Show him what you're made of."

"Thank you, Mr. Profitt," she said, sticking her hand out the window. They shook hands as if they were old comrades. Maggie was reminded once more how good it felt to be touched. As before, she was reluctant to let go. Only when the tips of her fingers began to tingle did she pull away.

"Call me Jason," he said. "Only one thing. Don't turn off your engine until that guy agrees to give you a new battery." He chuckled. "You may never get this one started again. Good luck, Maggie."

She mumbled something that remotely sounded like good-bye, then almost stalled her engine in her rush to get away. Only then did she realize how badly her palms were perspiring. Yes, it was definitely menopause. How else could she explain her rapid pulse, the hot flashes? Either that or she was losing her mind.

Jason watched the white station wagon cross the parking lot and disappear into the night traffic. He smiled as he thought of the woman driving it. He had never seen prettier green eyes. It irritated him that a man like Billy-Boy Friend could take advantage of such a woman. Especially a single parent who probably had a hard time making ends meet. But that was none of his business. Maggie Farnsworth was a grown woman and could take care of herself. He was letting those green eyes and shapely legs cloud his judgment.

Shrugging, Jason leaned over, retrieved the battery cables, and made his way toward the trunk of his car. Only then did he notice he was still holding Maggie's warranty.

Maggie's jaw was set at a determined angle as she marched across the parking lot of Friend's Automotive with her son beside her. "I'm going to prove to Mr. Friend, once and for all, that he's not dealing with a wimp." She held the door open for her son to pass through first.

Billy-Bob Friend stood behind a counter, picking his teeth and watching a Barbara Walters special on a small black-and-white portable. He glanced up as Maggie came in, took one look at her, and frowned. "Oh, it's you again," he said, not bothering to remove the toothpick.

"Damn right it is," she said, planting her hands squarely on her hips. She was mad now. Really mad. She had primed herself for this confrontation on the drive over, and she was determined not to back down. "My battery quit on me again."

The man merely shrugged and turned back to his program. "You musta left your lights on."

Maggie closed the distance between them. "You know darn good and well I didn't. You sold me a worthless battery, Mr. Friend, and I demand a new one." When he didn't so much as look her way, she pounded her fist on the counter. "Are you listening to me?"

He turned to her with a bored expression. "Lady, you can demand till the cows come home, but I ain't gonna replace it. You women just don't know how to take care of a car."

Maggie folded her arms over her chest and tapped her foot. "I'm not leaving this store until you give me a new battery. You'll either have to throw me out or call the police."

He sighed. "Look, lady, it's been a long day, okay? Why don't you come back in the morning, and we'll talk it over?"

She knew he was lying. It was just another stall tactic. Sooner or later she would give up and buy another battery. At least that's what he was counting on. He obviously didn't know how broke she was. Broke and stubborn. "If I have to come back tomorrow, it'll be to picket this place."

Billy-Bob looked confused. "What are you talking about?"

"It just so happens I know a lot of people in this town," she said, sticking her face right in his. "Now, you either give me a new battery, or I'll be here bright and early tomorrow with my son's Cub Scout pack and the peewee soccer team. I'll stay up all night making signs if I have to, telling folks how you cheated me."

The man studied her as though trying to decide whether or not she was serious. "You wouldn't do that."

Maggie hitched her chin high, her eyes challenging him. "Just try me."

The two glared at each other for a moment. They didn't hear the front door open or see the man stalk in. "Okay, lady, you can have your blasted battery," Billy-Bob said.

Maggie was prevented from gloating when someone stepped in front of her. She glanced up in surprise, then in outright shock as Jason Profitt pressed his wide hands on the counter and regarded Billy-Bob. "Remember me?" he said.

Billy-Bob muttered a string of cuss words. "Yeah, I remember you. You're that troublemaker who made such a fuss over them tires I sold you." He glanced from one to the other. "What is this, customers-from-hell night?"

"Damn right," Jason said. "Now, you get out from behind that counter and get this lady a new battery, or I'm going to make you eat her old one."

Billy-Bob didn't take his eyes off Jason as he rounded the counter and stood before him. "I think I'd like to see you try that, mister."

Maggie sucked her breath in sharply at the sight. Jason Profitt was the last person she'd expected to see. Billy-Bob towered over him by a good six inches. "Uh, Jason, I can take care of this," she said. She reached for his arm, but he shrugged her off.

"Stay back, Maggie, in case I have to use force."

That was the last thing that came out of Jason's mouth. Billy-Bob reared his fist back and struck him solidly in the face. Maggie winced at the bone-crunching sound and pulled Davey back, just as Jason fell backward onto a stack of tires. She screamed and ran to him.

"He's out cold," Billy-Bob said, dusting his hands off and giving a self-satisfied smile. "Now, let me get that battery."

Two

"Ouch!"

Maggie jumped back, almost dropping the ice pack. "I'm sorry, but I have to put this on your eye to get the swelling down."

Jason put tentative fingers to his cheekbone. "What'd he hit me with, a sledgehammer?"

"It was just his fist," she said. "But it was a *big* fist."

"Why didn't you tell me he'd agreed to give you a new battery before I barged in and threatened him?"

"You never gave me a chance."

Davey looked from Jason to his mother. "Boy, he really gave you wings, Coach. You almost *flew* across the store into that stack of tires."

Jason regarded the boy as Maggie put the ice pack to his bruise once more. The corners of his lips twitched with a show of humor. "Was it a graceful fall?"

Davey shook his head. "Not especially."

Maggie tried to stifle her laughter. She liked the fact that Jason was able to poke fun at himself.

"But it was a very macho sort of fall, wasn't it, Davey?"

Jason turned up his smile a notch. Amusement flickered in his eyes. "You're just trying to soothe my wounded ego. How long was I unconscious?"

"No more than a few seconds," she said. "You came to when Mr. Friend poured that cup of water in your face." At first Maggie had been horrified and insisted on taking Jason to the emergency room. They had argued back and forth over it while Billy-Bob Friend had carried out one of his top-of-the-line batteries and installed it in her car. He'd looked relieved to see them go.

"I had forgotten how big he was," Jason muttered.

"Well, I have a new battery now, so it worked out after all." Maggie paused and studied the nasty bruise above Jason's left cheekbone. "Except that you're going to have one heck of a shiner tomorrow," she added, feeling guilty because she was the cause of his injury. It was all her fault for driving off without her warranty, *her* fault for dragging him into her problems to begin with. Which is why she had insisted he follow her home so she could nurse him.

"Why don't you hold this ice pack in place, and I'll make us some coffee," Maggie suggested after a moment. Nice as it was touching the man, she'd decided enough was enough. Her legs hadn't stopped shaking since he had rushed into that automotive store like a modern-day Sir Galahad, since she had held him in her arms and waited for him to regain consciousness and wondered what it would be like to kiss him or *be* kissed by him. Jason nodded and reached for the pack, his knuckles brushing her hand. Startled, Maggie snatched the hand away, then blushed for overreacting. She faced her son, hoping to hide her discomfort from Jason, at the same time knowing she wasn't very successful. She could feel his gaze on her by the prickling of hairs on the back of her neck. "Time for your bath, young man," she said, thinking she sounded quite calm and composed despite the fact that Jason was playing havoc with her emotions.

"Aw, Mom! I wanted to stay and talk to the coach."

It was obvious the boy had gotten attached to the man in a short period of time. Maggie didn't know whether that was good or bad. All she knew was Davey desperately needed a friend at the moment, and Jason seemed content to spend a little time with him. Of course, it was up to her to see that Davey didn't take advantage of the man's generosity. "Your coach needs to rest if he's going to get better," she said. "Now, hurry along, and I'll make you a snack afterward." Reluctantly, Davey plodded in the direction of the bathroom, leaving them alone for the first time.

"Is your headache any better?" Maggie asked Jason as she put the coffee on and waited for it to drip through. It seemed to take forever, and she had nothing to do until it finished except stand there and stare at the man.

He nodded. "The aspirin helped. I don't usually take painkillers, you understand," he added. "I mean, I try to get by without that sort of thing."

"Well, this is different," she said, wondering why he was making excuses for taking medicine.

"What I'm trying to say is, I have an unusually high tolerance for pain."

She nodded. "I'm sure you do."

Jason chuckled. "What I'm *really* trying to do is hide my embarrassment. Here I was, determined to make Billy-Bob give you a new battery, and I ended up on the floor."

Maggie offered him a kind smile. She was touched by his honesty. "Nobody has ever done something like that for me."

His expression was sheepish. "Made a fool of himself?"

"Taken up for me the way you did." She thought of her ex-husband, who would have taken his business elsewhere instead of confronting a man like Billy-Bob Friend.

Jason removed the ice pack. "So how do I look?"

Maggie longed to tell him he was the best-looking thing she'd seen in a long time. But she didn't. And when she spoke, she tried to make her voice sound casual, as though it were an everyday event for her to have a good-looking man sitting at her table. "You're going to be bruised for a couple of days, but you'll live." She smiled as she carried a cup of coffee to him and set it down.

Jason thanked her, then as she turned and made her way to the counter, stole another quick glance at her legs. This time he allowed himself a closer inspection of her pert behind as well, adjusting the ice pack to get a better look. He liked what he saw. "You wouldn't be ashamed to be seen with me in public, would you?" he asked after a moment.

"Of course not." Maggie was half tempted to tell him how it would take a *lot* more than a black eye to detract from his good looks. At the same time, she was intrigued by the question. Perhaps even hunks were insecure from time to time.

Jason grinned. "Good. I figured maybe you could have dinner with me tomorrow night to celebrate your new battery and all," he said. Then, when she merely stared at him as though he'd lost his mind, he tried another approach. "And to sort of make up for letting that brute hurt me," he added.

"Dinner?" Maggie hadn't even seen it coming. But then, it was probably obvious to him from the way her mouth was hanging open.

"We could go somewhere dark. Maybe my bruises wouldn't stand out as much."

She wanted to tell him how little the bruises mattered to her. But dinner?

"You *are* ashamed to be seen with me, aren't you?" he said when she didn't answer right away.

"Ashamed? Oh, no. It's just—" She paused and grappled for a good excuse. "I don't have a sitter."

"Do you think you could find someone by tomorrow night? I'll pay, of course."

"Well, it's such short notice. And on a Saturday night. If it were any other night—"

He shrugged. "Then why don't I bring something here?" he said. "I could pick up a pizza or a bucket of chicken." Until that moment he hadn't realized how much he wanted to see her again. She was so different from the women he was used to, the model-thin sophisticates his mother fixed him up with and whose main concern in life was being seen with Jared Profitt's son by all the right people.

"Here?" Maggie said in a voice that suggested she found the thought about as appealing as dining beside a mosquito-infested swamp. No, that was definitely out of the question. "Oh, you don't want to come here," she assured him.

"I don't?" He looked amused.

It was on the tip of her tongue to tell him no. *No,* she couldn't have dinner with him. *No,* she didn't want him there either. It was such an easy thing to say; in fact, she said it all the time. Which was why, as Cynthia so charmingly put it, she had no life.

Darn, but she hated to say no to him. He seemed so different from the rest of the men she'd dated. Different in a nice way. He hadn't asked her how long she'd been divorced, whether or not she was lonely or had a man in her life and, if not, how she dealt with all those pent-up desires. That was the odd thing about being divorced, she had discovered. Folks assumed you weren't truly happy or complete unless you had a man in your bed.

Still, as nice as Jason was, she couldn't imagine what they would have in common. He was a bachelor; she a divorced parent. Not only that, she was older.

Heck, three years was nothing. Besides, this was the guy who'd stood up to Billy-Bob. This was the man who was going to make it possible for her son to play goalie. The least she could do was have dinner with him.

"Maggie?"

"I'll go!" She was almost relieved to have made the decision.

Jason looked both surprised and delighted. "Great." He drained his coffee cup and stood. "I'll pick you up at eight."

Maggie was already beginning to wonder if she had made a mistake by accepting. What would they talk about? "Eight is fine," she said instead.

Jason nodded. "Well, I'd better go. You'll say good night to Davey for me?"

Maggie assured him she would as she walked him to the door and waited for him to climb into his snazzy car, all the while praying that her ex-husband wouldn't show up and embarrass her before she'd had a chance to tell Jason a few things. A few *pertinent* things. Lord, what had she gotten herself into? Better yet, what had she gotten poor Jason into? Finally, he backed his car out of the driveway, and she was able to take her first breath of relief.

"What do you mean, you're not going?" Cynthia demanded. "You can't back out *now*, for Pete's sake!"

Maggie fidgeted with her hands as she paced her living room. It was already ten after eight, and there was no sign of Jason Profitt. Maybe he wasn't going to show after all, she told herself, half hoping that was the case. He'd save them both a lot of embarrassment. "Cynthia, you know darn good and well why I can't go," she whispered, not wanting her children to hear. Not that it was likely they'd hear *anything* with all the noise they were making upstairs. "I should have told him the truth last night."

"Don't you think you're blowing this whole thing out of proportion?"

"I've tried calling him all day," Maggie went on as though she hadn't heard a word, "but there was no answer. Maybe he had an emergency and had to leave town at the last minute. Maybe he found a better offer."

Cynthia gave a snort of disgust. "Would you listen to yourself! What man in his right mind would walk away from the chance to go out with you? Just look at you."

Maggie knew she looked especially nice in a black coat-dress with shiny gold buttons that matched her earrings. She'd had it on layaway for four months. Not only was Maggie wearing her nicest outfit, but Cynthia had spent a good hour and a half doing her hair and makeup. Boy, she was really going to feel crummy if Jason stood her up.

Maggie was about to break the sad news to her friend, when she heard a car pull up in her driveway. She peered out the tiny window in the door. "It's him!" she said, shock mingling with disbelief.

"So, go!" Cynthia grabbed Maggie's small clutch bag from the hall chest and thrust it at her. "Listen to me, Maggie Farnsworth," she said. "I don't often give up a Saturday night to baby-sit for someone else's kids, so you'd better get out there and have a good time." She opened the door and shoved her out.

Maggie stumbled out onto the porch, almost losing her balance in the process, then whirled around on high heels as the door slammed and the dead bolt clicked home. Her mouth flew open as realization hit. Cynthia had locked her out of her own house!

"I see you're ready to go."

Maggie spun around. All at once she found herself looking into Jason Profitt's handsome face. "Hi," she said, blushing so badly her ears burned. She would see that Cynthia paid for this. In the meantime she would try to salvage what dignity she had left. She toyed with her purse. "Your eye looks better." And it did. With the swelling down, the bruises near his cheekbone didn't look so bad. But she was grasping for something to say because she had never been in such a predicament.

"Hi, yourself," he said as though it were an everyday occurrence for his date to leap out the front door like an overzealous jackrabbit. He boldly assessed her and smiled, obviously liking what he saw. Her pulse raced. "You look great." He offered her his arm and escorted her to the car.

"You'll have to forgive the way I'm dressed," he said, suddenly realizing he was dressed much too casually. "There was a problem at work this afternoon, and I had to go in. I just got out of there." He paused. "Would you mind if we stopped by my apartment long enough for me to shower and change? I'll call the restaurant and let them know we're going to be late."

Maggie decided things were moving much too fast for her. First she had thought Jason was going to stand her up. Then as soon as he appeared, she'd been locked out of her own house. Now here he was trying to convince her to go home with him so he could change clothes. *Go home with him!* "Is this a line?" she blurted out.

"A line?" he asked, two light brown brows arching high.

She met his blue-eyed gaze and thought she found humor there. "Well, I haven't dated much lately, so I'm wondering if this is what guys say these days to lure unsuspecting females into their apartments." Although there was a teasing lilt in her voice, she wanted him to know she was not in the habit of going home with strange men, especially her son's soccer coach.

"I assure you this is no line," he said. "I just want to shower and change. We can leave the front door open if you like. Better yet, I'll show you all my Boy Scout badges. You know you can trust a Boy Scout." When she didn't look convinced, he went on. "And your baby-sitter knows you're going out with me, doesn't she? I'd be a fool to try anything."

"You probably think I'm being silly," she said as she let him lead her to his car.

He shook his head. "Not at all," he told her. "As a single parent, you have to be careful."

If only he knew, she thought.

"I'm glad you could come, Maggie," Jason said once he'd climbed in beside her and pulled his car onto the main road. "I haven't gone out much since I started my new job." The sound of his voice, rich and husky and sensual, made her feel as breathless as if she had run a relay race.

"How'd you end up coaching soccer?" she asked, having wanted to ask that question from the beginning. She could see him in a fashionable singles bar or a gym, but she could not imagine a man like Jason coaching soccer, especially when he had no children of his own.

He chuckled. "One of the guys at work talked me into it. I used to play as a kid." He shrugged. "Anyway, I figured the fresh air and exercise would do me good. Had I known I was going to meet a pretty redhead, I would have done this sort of thing a long time ago." He winked, and Maggie totally lost her place in the conversation.

Ten minutes later Jason turned into a new apartment complex that catered to single and young married professionals. As he paused to unlock his door, Maggie studied her surroundings. The complex was tucked in a wooded section and gave one the feeling of being far from the city. The advertisements she'd seen for the place boasted an Olympic-size pool and several tennis courts as well as a spacious clubhouse for parties and other gatherings. Children and pets weren't allowed. Which explained why it was so quiet and serene, like something out of one of those glamorous perfume commercials where the women were thin and tan and the men muscle-bound.

Maggie watched a young couple garbed in white

make their way toward the tennis courts, swinging their racquets and laughing to themselves and looking as though they were on an extended vacation. Maggie couldn't remember when she'd felt so out of place. Had she ever been young and carefree? she wondered. As much as she loved her children, she couldn't remember a time when she had been able to come and go as she pleased. She'd always had to look after someone. Before her children had come along, it had been her mother and her younger sister. For the most part, though, she enjoyed caring for others. It made her feel loved and needed.

Still, she hadn't done enough as far as her ex-husband, Bob, was concerned. He'd ended up leaving her. Even though there were extenuating circumstances, Maggie felt she had failed him and her children miserably.

She had promised herself, never again.

So what was she doing with Jason Profitt!

"A penny for your thoughts," he said as he held the door to his apartment open and waited for her to pass through.

Maggie glanced up, startled she had been so pensive. "I'm sorry," she said, faltering for a reply. "I guess I'm just a little nervous."

"Relax, Maggie. You have absolutely nothing to be nervous about. I want you to enjoy an evening out, okay?"

She decided she liked the way he said her name, soft and husky, making the skin on the back of her neck tingle. Maggie smiled as she stepped into Jason's apartment. "Oh, this is lovely," she said, taking in the decor. It smacked of money with its Persian rugs and leather sofas and original paintings of wildlife scenes. A solid mahogany wall unit held an expensive-looking stereo system, a widescreen TV, and an impressive selection of books, all bound in leather.

"My mother decorated it," he said without much emotion. "Have a seat. I'll pour you a glass of wine while I call the restaurant." He hurried into the next room.

Maggie sat on the sofa and waited for Jason. She couldn't help but notice that everything looked brand-new and very nice compared to her own furniture. There wasn't a single handprint to be found on the walls.

"Here we go," Jason said, coming into the room a few minutes later with a filled wineglass. He handed it to her. "I promise I'll hurry," he said. "There are plenty of magazines you can read while I'm in the shower," he added before disappearing again.

Maggie thumbed through an *Architectural Digest* and sipped her wine. She heard the sound of running water from somewhere in the apartment. After a moment she stood and walked to a large sliding glass door and peeked through one of the vertical blinds. The pool and clubhouse were only a short distance away, surrounded by neat flower beds. Although it was too cold for swimming, couples lounged nearby, beneath a crisp green and white striped cabana, talking and sipping frothy drinks. There wasn't a kid in sight. Neither were there scattered toys or hopscotch boards or forgotten bicycles. She might as well have been on a different planet, as much as it resembled her life.

Maggie had finished her glass of wine by the time Jason came out of the bedroom. He looked wonderful in a pair of khaki slacks, white dress shirt, and navy sport jacket. The smile he gave her took her breath away. "See, that didn't take very long, now, did it?"

"Jason, we have to talk," Maggie said. The wine had made her feel brave, and she had a few things to get off her chest.

He checked his pockets for keys and wallet, and it was obvious he was in a hurry. "Sure." Then, glancing at his wristwatch, he added, "Can we talk in the car? We have only ten minutes to get to the restaurant."

Maggie nodded and let him escort her out the door and into his car again. Once on the road, though, he was forced to concentrate on his driving. It looked as though every teenager in Crescent City was out cruising tonight.

They arrived at the restaurant, where a pleasant hostess led them to a secluded table at the back of the dining room. "I hear this place has great food," Jason said once they were seated, "but you can't get in on a Saturday night without a reservation."

Jason ordered them each a cocktail, then leaned back in his chair and sighed happily while the waiter went to get their drinks. "I can't tell you how good it feels to get out, Maggie," he said. "It sort of makes up for the past two months and all the work I've had to do. I suppose you know what hard work is, though, don't you? Being a single parent and all."

This was her chance, Maggie thought. She would come clean with him, let him know that she hadn't been totally honest. It was only fair she level with him before he spent a lot of money on a nice meal. "Uh, Jason?"

"All I want to do tonight is relax and gaze across the table at my pretty date," he said. "I don't want to think about my job or worry about anything else. What d'you say, Maggie? It's just you and me tonight, and the rest of the world can wait."

She was about to respond, when the waiter returned with two strawberry daiquiris. "I'd like to make a toast," Jason said as soon as the man walked away. He pondered a moment, then held his glass high. "To new towns and new friends." He winked. "I can already tell I'm going to like Crescent City a lot."

Maggie met his warm gaze over the candle and smiled. Finally, she raised her glass to his and took a sip of her drink. "This is scrumptious," she said, licking her bottom lip.

Jason's eyes followed her pink tongue as it flicked a drop of the frothy drink from the corner of her mouth. Scrumptious was the word he would have used to describe *her,* he decided. Her coral lips were full and tempting; her eyes spar-kled like city lights. In the glow of the candle, her hair was a rich auburn color. "I was afraid you were going to renege on our date," he said. "Most women wouldn't be excited about going out with a guy with a black eye."

His gaze was as soft as a caress. Maggie felt she was being pulled toward him on a slow but steady current. "It's not as noticeable tonight."

"That's only because it's so dark in here. Why do you think I was so worried about losing our reservation? I didn't want to end up in a fast-food restaurant with bright lighting."

They chatted for a moment over their drinks. Jason told Maggie about his new job, and she told him about her job as secretary at the textile plant on the edge of town.

"Do you like it?" he asked.

"I'm not crazy about my boss, but it pays better than most jobs around here, so I stay."

Maggie was shocked at the prices when the waiter handed them menus.

"Order anything you like, Maggie," Jason said, noting the uncertainty in her eyes. "Of course, the people at work recommend the prime rib. What d'you say we both order that?"

Maggie nodded. She couldn't remember when she'd last eaten a gourmet meal. She suddenly felt like Cinderella. Surely she wouldn't be considered a terrible mother if she enjoyed herself for one night. After all, how many times had she refused to go to lunch with friends at work because she couldn't afford the cost of a restaurant? Instead, she ate her bologna sandwich and drank the free coffee offered at work because she refused to pay sixty-five cents for a soft drink. Tonight she would forget all that. She would simply enjoy herself and the food, not to mention the handsome man sitting across the table from her.

The waiter came and took their order, then disappeared again, leaving them to enjoy the candlelight and piano music coming from the next room. When he started serving the food fifteen minutes later, Maggie couldn't help but wonder if he would ever stop. There was a crisp garden salad with her favorite bleu cheese dressing that she seldom bought for herself at home because her children preferred French. There was hot baked bread with butter, stuffed potatoes, baby carrots, and a thick slice of prime rib cooked just the way she liked it. By the time she'd finished half her meat she was full and didn't feel the least bit shy about requesting to take home her leftovers. She turned down Jason's offer of dessert, choosing to sip a cup of cinnamon-flavored coffee instead. Still, he insisted she have a bite of the blueberry cheesecake he'd ordered as they shared stories of growing up.

Jason told her what it was like to live in a place like West Palm Beach, where there were no seasons, where Christmas lights were often draped on palm trees instead of evergreens. He told her what it was like to attend an all-male boarding school and be labeled the class prankster.

"I hated that school," he said, "and I tried to punish my parents by staying in trouble. In the end I won, and they allowed me to come home." He chuckled. "Remember this, Maggie," he said. "If Davey ever gives you a hard time, send him to a military academy."

Maggie smiled as he said it, but after hearing about his boyhood, she was reminded once more how little they had in common.

"Oh, look at the time," she said, glancing at her wristwatch suddenly and discovering it was already after eleven o'clock. She looked around at the near-empty restaurant. "I had no idea it was so late." She hadn't even bothered to check on her children.

Jason looked equally surprised. "Yeah, I guess I was enjoying myself so much, I lost track." He motioned for the check, and Maggie couldn't help but notice the tip he left the waiter more than made up for their staying so late.

Linking his fingers through hers, Jason led Maggie from the restaurant to his car. The night air was cool on her face, a direct contrast to the warmth emanating from Jason's wide palm and sturdy fingers. She shivered. Not from the cold, but from the feel of him.

Jason paused beside the car long enough to unlock her door. "Are you cold?" he asked, squeezing her hand slightly.

She met his gaze. His eyes looked liquid in the moonlight. "I like it," she said. "Fall and winter are my favorite seasons."

"Why is that, Maggie?" he asked with a smile. He wanted to know more about her. He wanted to know her likes and dislikes, her dreams and goals, her secret desires.

He'd used her name again. It sounded so different when he said it in that velvet-edged voice of his, that voice that was as soothing to her senses as it was disconcerting. "I don't know. Maybe because it brings families closer together," she said. "The weather turns cold and forces everybody inside to warm fires and thick soups and hot chocolate. It's snuggling weather," she added with a smile, then thought how nice it would be to snuggle up with him. She felt a warm blush on her body just thinking about it. "And then there are the holidays, of course."

Jason gazed down at Maggie, mesmerized. She was plain, really, not the drop-dead-gorgeous sort of creature men lost their heads over. But watching the play of emotions on her face, he thought she was the most beautiful woman he'd ever seen. She made him feel warm inside. He stepped closer, slipping his arms around her waist. Her green eyes registered surprise. She was not someone who hid her emotions well, he thought. Perhaps that's why he liked her so much.

"I have to kiss you, Maggie," he whispered, smiling gently. "You're too sweet to resist."

Maggie barely had time to process the information before Jason lowered his head and captured her lips. His mouth was full and tasted of the dessert he'd eaten earlier. His body was solid and warm against hers, sending a ripple of awareness through her. As he parted her lips with an eager tongue, Maggie leaned into the embrace, giving in, not only to the taste and scent of him but also the comforting heat. Already she could feel her body responding to him, to the warmth and power of his touch. But her body had been responding to him all night. She felt it in her tingling limbs.

Raising his head slightly, Jason could only gaze down at Maggie, his heart in his throat. He wanted to go on kissing her. But even he knew it wouldn't be enough. He could already feel the urgent stirrings low in his belly. He wanted to make love to her, then hold her while she slept. He wanted to be the first one to gaze into her sleepy eyes come morning.

"I'd better take you home," he said, realizing the physical contact had left him more than a little shaken. What had started out innocently enough had turned into something powerful and totally unexpected.

Maggie tried to make light conversation on the drive home, but tension shrouded them like a heavy curtain.

One kiss had changed everything.

The easygoing camaraderie they had shared all evening was gone, replaced now with an uncomfortable awareness that alternately thrilled and terrified her. She saw the changes in his face, the furtive glances he gave her. She felt it in the sexually charged air. It crackled with expectancy. The lights from the dashboard cast a soft glow in the front seat, and Maggie felt as if she were glowing too.

"Maggie?"

The sound of his voice in the still car made her jump as though a rifle had exploded in the seat next to her. One hand flew to her chest as though she half feared her heart would leap out.

"Sorry if I startled you."

She laughed to hide her embarrassment. "I'm just jumpy tonight," she confessed.

He chuckled, rich throaty laughter that sent tiny shivers along her spine. "Me too," he said. "Wonder why?"

"I don't know." Liar, she thought.

He reached for her hand, squeezed it once, then raised it to his lips and pressed a kiss against her open palm. "I think you do, Maggie darlin'."

The unexpected endearment struck a familiar chord in her body, a sense of longing that had been with her for as long as she could remember, since before her divorce. It frightened her. She pulled her hand away, but she could still feel the imprint of his lips against her palm. She made a fist in her lap, hoping to keep his kiss with her a few more minutes before letting it go.

"I want to see you again, Maggie."

The way he said it, calm and matter-of-fact, told Maggie he meant it. Her stomach tensed; she felt an odd mixture of hope and fear. But despite all her apprehension, she felt a deep joy. She gazed out her window at the black night, waiting for her heart to stop jumping in her chest. "I don't know, Jason," she said after a moment. "I had a wonderful time tonight, but—"

"But what?" There was alarm in his voice. After the wonderful time they'd had, he could not imagine why she wouldn't be as eager as he was to be together again.

"You don't even know me," she said with a light chuckle. This time she looked at him. His own look was one of confusion and disbelief.

"I know I want to see more of you."

"Why don't we sleep on it, Jason," she said. "We can talk tomorrow." Her suggestion brought a frown to his face, but Maggie didn't have time to worry about it. He had already turned into her subdivision, and that brought to mind the details she had failed to mention about herself. Lord knew they had talked about everything else.

Maggie gripped the door handle as Jason rounded a corner and turned down her street. She could feel him watching her, questioning the changes that had taken place in her since that kiss. The best thing she could do at this point was say good-night *quickly* and get out of the car, she told herself. The following day she would call him and tell him the truth, if it was the last thing she did. She had been wrong to hold back information, although holding back had become such an integral part of her personality. She had learned the less you gave of yourself, the less chance you took of being hurt. But she had been wrong to hold back in this case and pretend she was something she was not. Jason Profitt was a nice guy and didn't deserve deception. Yes, she would call him the next day and tell him the truth. Over the phone she wouldn't have to gaze into those dreamy eyes and inhale his tangy after-shave. She wouldn't have to worry about him kissing her again and sending her into a tizzy.

Jason had managed to get only halfway down her street before Maggie noticed every light in her house was burning. He pulled into the driveway, and she blinked in surprise as she watched a number of shadows pass before the curtains. Children running. She panicked. Everything else was forgotten.

"Something's wrong!" she said, opening the door and climbing out of Jason's car before he could turn off the engine. She literally flew up the walk, her heart pounding so loud she didn't hear Jason behind her. She heard a scream from inside and almost tore the door off its hinges.

Cynthia was the first to see her. "Oh, thank God you're home!" she said, her hand flying to her heart. "You won't believe what happened."

Maggie was breathing hard as she took in the scene before her. Her daughters were standing on the sofa, arms flailing, screaming to the top of their lungs. "What is it?" she asked breathlessly.

From the hall she could hear Davey laughing; loud, raucous laughter that made absolutely no sense when compared to the terror-stricken faces of his sisters. He doubled over when he spotted Maggie and Jason standing there. "Guess what?" he said. "King Solomon got out of his cage and everybody is going berserk around here 'cause I can't find him."

Maggie stood totally still for a moment, not knowing what to say. She had already done a head count and was relieved to find everybody in one piece. Her relief was short-lived when Jason stepped closer, his face masked in surprise and confusion.

"Who is King Solomon?" he asked.

Maggie felt her heart plummet to her stomach. She didn't quite meet his look. "Davey's pet snake," she said. "He's harmless, of course. Just ugly and slithery."

Jason nodded. Taking in the scene, he added, "I didn't know you had company."

This time Maggie faced him. The color had drained from her face. "This isn't company, Jason. These are my children." His mouth fell open in disbelief, and she knew a moment of intense disappointment. He was going to react to her news the way every other man had. "Yes, you heard me right," she went on without waiting for a reply.

"It's not a pajama party or my Sunday school class. They belong to me. Count them, Jason. Five. Four girls and one boy."

"You have five children?" he sputtered.

"Yes. That's seven less than an equal dozen." She sighed heavily. "And the reason I didn't tell you is that I knew *exactly* the kind of look you'd give me when I did. Well, I want you to know, Jason Profitt, I *chose* to have a big family. I guess this means I'll be seeing you around, huh? No, let me guess: You've got to go now, right? And you'll be *calling* me." Maggie was so caught up in her tirade that she didn't notice the odd looks Cynthia and her children were giving her. The snake seemed to have been forgotten for the time being.

She had not realized how loudly she'd been talking, but now that she'd stopped, the room was suddenly quiet. Not a person moved.

And then, all at once, Jason started to laugh. "Well, there's something to be said for this situation. At least you don't live in a shoe." Then he doubled over with laughter.

Three

Maggie stood rooted to her spot as Jason took in the scene with a great deal of amusement. A *great* deal of amusement.

"He seems to be taking it well," she told Cynthia.

"Either that or he's hysterical. Are his eyes dilated?"

"I can't tell. He's not clutching his chest, though, like the last guy." Maggie stepped closer to him. "Jason, listen to me," she said. "You have every right to be shocked or angry with me for not telling you sooner. I wouldn't blame you if you never wanted to see me again."

Finally, Jason stopped laughing. "Maggie, is that why you acted so strange on the drive back?" When she nodded, he went on. "I mean, I could tell something was bothering you, but I couldn't figure out what it was. I thought we were hitting it off so well."

His gaze was so riveting, she had to look away. "Well, yes."

"What a relief!"

She and Cynthia exchanged looks. "Relief?" she said, chancing another glance in his direction.

"Yes. I thought I had said or done something wrong."

"You mean it doesn't bother you that I have five children?" she asked.

"Not in the least." He chuckled. "I'm crazy about kids. Now, move out of my way so I can help Davey find his snake." He was still laughing under his breath as he disappeared down the hall, leaving the two women staring at each other openmouthed. Cynthia was the first to speak. "If I were you, I'd handcuff that man to my bed and never let him go."

Twenty minutes later Jason and Davey had returned King Solomon to his glass cage, and they were all gathered around the large kitchen table for milk and cookies, during which time Jason insisted Maggie introduce her children.

"This is Jessie, my oldest," she said, motioning to a girl who was the image of herself. "She's thirteen." Maggie waited until Jason and her daughter shook hands. "And these are my twins, Amber and Beth. They're eleven." She smiled at the girls. "As you can see, they're identical. Which makes for a lot of confusion." She turned toward her youngest. "The one with the milk mustache is Molly. She just turned five."

"She's spoiled," one of the twins said.

"Rotten to the core," Jessie supplied.

Maggie grinned. "And you know Davey, of course."

Jason nodded. "Of course. My star goalie." He smiled and winked at the boy, and when he faced Maggie once more his eyes still held the warmth of that smile. "You have a nice family."

"Nice and big," she said. "Most people are overwhelmed when they see us all together. It scares them."

He knew she was feeling him out. He could read the wariness, the vulnerability in her eyes. She expected him to bolt. Suddenly, all he wanted to do was cup her face in his hands and kiss her doubts away. But he couldn't. Not with her children watching his every move. All he could do was gaze into those emerald eyes of hers and answer as honestly as he could. "I'm not most people, and I don't scare easily," he said.

For a moment Maggie was unable to do more than stare back at him in wide-eyed disbelief. Something passed between them, some indefinable emotion that pulled her to him with the subtleness of an undertow hidden beneath a fast-moving current. Although it lasted only an instant, it was powerful and real and made her head spin as though she had just taken a wild carnival ride. With a great deal of effort Maggie dragged her attention away from him and faced her children. She felt her sense of normalcy return. "Okay now, it's after midnight. Everybody to bed."

There was a chorus of protests, but Maggie insisted. "Wait here," she told Jason as she herded the group upstairs. She returned a few minutes later and found him sitting on her sofa, looking thoughtful.

"We need to talk," he said.

Maggie felt a sinking sensation in the pit of her stomach as she joined him on the sofa, sitting at a respectable distance. He looked so serious, she knew it had to be bad. Perhaps he was having second thoughts.

"Why didn't you tell me?" he said.

Maggie did not need clarification. "Like I said earlier, it scares most people?"

"You mean men?"

She nodded. "Not that I blame them. Raising children is no easy task. It's time-consuming and expensive, not to mention frustrating." It was her way of letting him know she completely understood his reluctance to get involved. He was off the hook, and she wasn't going to hold it against him.

"What about their father?"

She laughed. "He's kind of hard to pin down, I'm afraid. Once in a while he'll take the girls off my hands, but he has a hard time with Davey. I think the divorce hurt our son more than anybody."

"How long have you been divorced?"

"Four years. Molly was six months old when I filed the papers."

"What happened?"

She hesitated, wondering why he wanted to know, wondering why it should matter one way or the other. "I think having a wife and five kids got to be too much for him. In the beginning he wanted a big family as much as I did. But after Jessie the twins came along, and they were a handful." She chuckled. "Then I got pregnant with Davey, and I suddenly had no energy left at the end of the day. He was five weeks premature and came with a bunch of health problems. Nothing serious, but he was sick a lot in the beginning. We sort of decided that was enough." She paused. "Then I discovered I was pregnant with Molly. It happened purely by accident, but Bob flipped when I told him." She sighed and shook her head. "I mean, let's face it, I'm as fertile as good Mississippi soil." She blushed the minute the words left her mouth. Of all the things to say!

Jason resisted the urge to smile when he realized Maggie had embarrassed herself. Nevertheless, the mere mention of her fertileness sent a tremor of desire through him. It made him think of soft things, warm things. His eyes traveled automatically to her breasts, and he swallowed, then shifted uncomfortably on the sofa and forced his gaze away.

"You sound as though you blame yourself, Maggie," he said, his voice sounding unnatural and a bit strained in his own ears. "Don't forget it takes two to make a baby."

"That didn't matter to Bob. He wanted out regardless."

Jason pondered all he'd been told. "So where does this leave us, Maggie?" he asked, thinking it was time they changed the subject so his breathing could return to normal.

She was surprised he'd left it up to her. Most men never gave her a choice in the matter. A man took one look at her five kids, and the next thing she found herself looking at was his backside. "I can't risk going through something like that again, Jason."

"And you think it's inevitable?" He smiled gently. It was obvious she had been wounded in her previous relationship. He couldn't help but wonder about her ex-husband. What kind of man would turn his back on a woman and five children?

"I guess I do," she confessed. "It wasn't easy starting over. One day I just woke up and realized I was the only person I had left in the world to depend on. I wanted to pull the covers over my head and hide, but I couldn't. I decided then and there that I was never going to count on someone else." She was surprised that she was able to tell him these things about herself. She wasn't one to just blurt out her feelings, but instinct told her they would be safe with Jason.

"You're not the first person to suffer a broken heart, Maggie."

"I know that. And I wouldn't be so reluctant to get involved again if it were only me I had to worry about. But it's not me by myself. I have to think of my children."

He sighed. "Okay, back to my original question. Where does that leave *us*? You and me?"

"I suppose we can still be friends." It sounded about as exciting as greasy dishwater.

"Friends?" He chuckled. "Isn't it a little late for that?"

She knew he was referring to their kiss. It was strange how she was so attuned to his thoughts and feelings, considering she hadn't known him very long. "We just got carried away," she said. "It won't happen again."

"What makes you so sure?"

She had no answer for that one, simply because she knew in her heart she wanted him to kiss her again. And the look he gave her told her he would be only too happy to comply. She could see it in his eyes, the way they lingered on her lips as though tasting them again in his mind. And each time he did it, she felt her own response low in her belly, a coiling tension, drawing and twisting her nerves tighter and tighter until it was impossible to think straight.

"We have nothing in common, Jason," she said, wanting to make him understand why it would be a mistake to get involved, at the same time reinforce it in her own mind. It wasn't easy. Each time she tried to detach herself from him, she caught a whiff of his after-shave or glimpsed those blue eyes and her resolve scattered like dry leaves in a strong wind. "I mean, here I am, divorced with a ready-made family, and you've never even been married. Not only that, you're three years younger than I."

"And you think all that matters?"

"It does to me."

Jason studied her, the stubborn tilt of her chin, the determined look in her eyes. It was ironic that she was the one pulling away. How many times had he tried to avoid a relationship because it didn't feel right? Which was why, at thirty years old, he'd never even come close to settling down with a woman. He wasn't so sure he liked having those same words aimed at him. Nor did he like having limits set.

"What makes you think I'd be willing to settle for friendship?" he asked.

Maggie saw the challenge in his eyes. She suspected Jason Profitt wasn't used to having someone else make the rules for him. And what woman wouldn't be more than willing to get to know him better? But she couldn't let herself be taken in by his charm and good looks. With five children to care for, she couldn't afford to lose her head over a confirmed bachelor.

"Friendship is all I have to offer at this time."

"At this time?"

She paused. "Well, if I ever *do* decide to get serious with a man, it will be with someone older and more stable. A *mature* man who won't mind taking on a ready-made family. I'm not looking to be swept off my feet, Jason," she added. "At my age, I'm more interested in security."

"At your age?" He looked amused. "Thirty-three doesn't exactly make you a candidate for Medicare, Maggie darlin'." He moved closer. "And you know what? I think this is all a crock. I think you *do* want to be swept off your feet." She started to object, but he silenced her, placing an index finger against her lips. "You're just too damn scared and stubborn to admit it." He slid closer still, so close, his thigh pressed into hers. Relaxing his finger on her mouth, he traced her full bottom lip. It quivered, and he felt it in his gut. "You can tell me all you want how you'd rather have security and stability in your life, but that's not *all* you want."

She brushed his hand away, but she could still feel the path he'd traced around her mouth. "You don't know what I want."

"Yes, I do. It's written all over your pretty face. I see it every time I look into those gorgeous green eyes. And when a man makes love to you, you want the earth to move."

She felt herself blushing, growing hot all over. Hot and tingly. Her knees trembled, and she was thankful she was sitting down. She hated the part of her that was so weak, the part of her that yearned to hear more of what he had to say. Sweet nothings. That's all they were. For no matter how good he made her feel or how many promises he made, if she were to make the monumental mistake of letting him spend a night in her bed, he would be gone in the morning, and she would be alone again. But, oh, how tempting it was. She had almost forgotten what it was like to be held by a man, to feel a man's bold caress, to lie against a man's wide chest.

"I suppose you think you're the man who can do these things for me," she said. Her tone was as stiff and unyielding as a metal pole. She couldn't let herself be swayed by softly spoken words or seductive phrases.

"I know I can. I knew it the minute I laid eyes on you. Why do you think I charged into that automotive store like a fool that first night? I knew even then that I wanted you. And tonight you proved you wanted me just as much. That kiss said it all, Maggie."

Her cheeks flared. She had heard enough. "Listen Jason, it's time we put an end to this conversation. You've no right to tell me what I want and need in my life. I'm thirty-three years old. Old enough to decide for myself. If I ever *do* decide to get involved again, which is very doubtful, it won't be with some young stud who doesn't know the first thing about family and commitment and responsibility."

"Young stud?" He didn't try to hide his surprise. "Is that how you see me, Maggie?" When she didn't answer, he stood. "Maybe I was wrong about you after all," he said. "I thought I saw life in your eyes. A yearning. But you're ready to wither up and die." He paused and his blue eyes looked sad. Sad but resigned. "I'd better go," he said, his tone matching the look on his face. He made his way to the front door and let himself out quietly.

Maggie continued to sit on the sofa for a few minutes, staring into space and pondering all that Jason had said. *You're ready to wither up and die.* Inside, she felt as though some part of her *already* had died. When had it happened? she wondered. When had she lost her zest, her exuberance for life? Then she realized that she hadn't even known she was missing those parts of her until Jason had managed to get inside her head and heart and make her see for herself. Somewhere along the way she had simply stopped living. She was merely going through the motions. With a heavy heart Maggie rose from the couch and began turning off the lights.

• • •

Maggie didn't expect to hear from Jason, and she didn't. Still, she was a nervous wreck when she took Davey to soccer practice the following Monday. She sat next to Cynthia on the bleachers and watched Jason work with her son on the field, and she tried not to remember the kiss they'd shared. And when Cynthia commented that Jason's shoulders were the broadest in three counties, she tried not to think about that either. Of course, Cynthia had asked about their date, but Maggie had shrugged it off, telling her that even though Jason was nice enough, they really didn't have much in common. For once Cynthia seemed to accept her explanation without asking a million questions.

Maggie was certain she had made the right decision by not encouraging a romantic relationship between her and Jason. In her four years as a divorcee, she had befriended other divorced women who, out of sheer loneliness, had not acted wisely and had lived to regret what their actions had done to them and to their children. She knew women who frequented singles bars and dated men who were no good for them, simply because they were tired of spending all their Saturday nights alone. Maggie had promised herself *never* to go that route, because in the end, her children would suffer the consequences. She'd stayed away from singles bars, married men, and dead-end relationships. Common sense told her she had done the right thing by discouraging Jason, and when Davey joined her after the game and announced his coach had appointed him goalie, Maggie fixed a big smile on her face and ushered the boy away quickly so she wouldn't have to face the man.

On Wednesday Maggie had to do it all over again, since Davey's practice games had been scheduled twice a week. This time Jason sought her out as soon as the game was over. Because Cynthia had had to leave early to meet a dinner date, Maggie waited alone for Davey and Abby to join her. She was standing beside the bleachers when Jason casually walked up to her, a soccer ball tucked under one arm.

"Can we talk?" he asked.

Maggie watched him take the ball between his hands, and her attention was drawn to his fingers. They were long and graceful, but masculine.

"That depends on what you have to say," she said, trying not to notice how good he looked. How young and virile. But then, he *would* look good. He had not given birth to five babies. He'd never sat up all night with a sick child or worried how he would buy five pairs of shoes and still afford groceries and the mortgage payment. He'd hurt her with that wither-and-die remark he'd made the other night. How the heck did he expect her to fit love and romance into her already hectic life? What did *he* know about responsibility and setting examples and establishing priorities?

"I'm sorry for the other night, Maggie," he said. "I was out of line."

She had not expected an apology, but it took some of the sting out of her anger. "Yes, you were," she said, meeting his gaze.

"I had a good time with you. I had planned to keep on seeing you until you backed off. I don't like others setting limits for me. Still, I can see why it's so important to keep your children from being hurt again." When she didn't reply, he went on. "That's why I've decided to go along with what you said. I'd rather be your friend than not see you at all." She looked faintly surprised. He chuckled. "That shouldn't surprise you, Maggie. We were friends almost from the beginning. I can't remember when I've enjoyed talking with someone as much as I did with you that night. I was as amazed as you when that kiss got out of control." He paused. "So what d'you say? Friends?" He offered his hand.

Maggie hesitated only a moment before she slipped her own hand into his. "Yes," she said. "Friends."

"Great." He squeezed her hand once before letting it go. "Now that we've got that settled, I'd like to have you come to my place Friday night for cocktails and hors d'oeuvres. Don't go getting that defensive look in your eyes," he said. "I'm having a few people over from work, and I don't have a date for the evening. But I'll be sure to let everyone know we're not a couple. I'll tell them you're a distant cousin or something, how's that?"

"I don't expect you to do that," she said. "As long as *we* know where we stand, that's enough."

"Right. Well, I have to go," he said, and rushed off without another word.

Maggie watched him leave, a perplexed frown drawing her eyebrows together as she thought about what he'd just said.

I was as amazed as you when that kiss got out of control.

Now, what in Sam Hill had he meant by *that* remark? And then it hit her. It was as obvious as the freckles on her nose. Jason Profitt did not see her as a passionate sort of woman. As nice as she was, it was not likely any man would lose his head over her and find himself pushed past his limits of self-control.

Maggie uttered a sound of disgust as she followed the two sweaty soccer players to the car. Well, Jason Profitt was wrong about her. She *wasn't* some withered old woman with one foot in the grave, and she had *plenty* of passion left in her body. And if Jason were anywhere near her type, she would show him. She would knock his socks off with all her pent-up passion!

Maggie came to an abrupt halt as she realized the direction her thoughts were taking. She pressed her hands against her cheeks and found them hot. Lord, she had to stop thinking about Jason and her unleashed passion. Otherwise, she'd never be able to drive home without running into something.

Four

Maggie almost didn't make it to Jason's party. First her boss kept her late at work. When she arrived home, Molly was frantic because her cat had climbed one of the tall pines out back and no amount of coaxing could get the animal to come down. The teenage baby-sitter who watched the children after school was more than a little irritated by Maggie's tardiness because she had a date that evening and wanted to leave. Maggie saw the girl off, then convinced her brood to come inside and have dinner, during which time the cat came out of the tree all by herself. Davey became visibly upset when he learned she was going to Jason's party when *he* hadn't been invited.

"It's an adult party," she explained. "He's just having a few friends from work."

"Then why are *you* going? You don't work with him."

Maggie was surprised that her son was so disagreeable about the whole thing. He hadn't minded her going to dinner with his coach that first time because, as he'd put it, "Jason's new in town and needs someone to show him around. Since I'm not allowed to stay up past ten, it's only right for my mother to go in my place." But he wasn't at all happy that he had not been invited to Jason's party, especially since it wasn't a school night and he was allowed to stay up later.

"I'm only going to help him serve his guests," Maggie said, trying to play down her importance. "And I'll probably get stuck doing the dishes afterward." She suspected that would take some of the sting out of his being excluded, and she was right. Davey suddenly lost all interest.

"I don't even feel like going now," Maggie confessed to Cynthia when she arrived. She was tired and frazzled and had no desire to spend the evening trying to be charming to a bunch of strangers.

"You'll feel better after you take a shower. Now, go." Cynthia offered her a stern look and pointed toward the bathroom.

"You're too good to me."

"No I'm not. I owe you for about two years worth of baby-sitting, if you'll remember."

"Yes, but you have only one child to my five."

Cynthia didn't look the least bit concerned. "I brought a couple of videos. That'll keep everybody quiet for a while."

A squarish, gray-haired man met Maggie at the front door of Jason's apartment when she arrived more than an hour late. "The name's Mort Holmes," he said, pumping her hand enthusiastically. "You must be Maggie. Jason's told me all about you." He opened the door wide. "Come on in. I'm supposed to look after you till Jason gets back with the ice."

Maggie followed him through a crowded living room, where men and women laughed and tried to make themselves heard over the music coming from Jason's elaborate stereo system. The dining room table was piled high with snacks and sandwiches.

"Name your poison," Mort said once they'd reached Jason's galleylike kitchen.

Maggie offered him a blank look. "I beg your pardon?"

"What'll you have to drink?"

"Oh. White wine, if you have it. Otherwise I'll just have a soft drink."

Mort checked the refrigerator. "Ah-ha, white wine coming up." He filled a plastic cup and handed it to her. "So tell me more about yourself, Maggie. Jason was right when he said you were pretty."

Maggie felt uncomfortable in the small kitchen, but she knew the rest of the apartment was equally crowded. Still, she was forced to stand too close to Mort. Why had Jason told him about her in the first place? she wondered as she took in the man's shiny gray slacks and wrinkled dress shirt. She took a sip of wine and wished Jason would get back.

"There's not much to tell, really," she said after a moment. She suddenly felt trapped, both by the man and his annoyingly sweet-scented aftershave. "Did Jason mention I have five children?" She hoped the news would put a little distance between them. It worked with most men.

Mort didn't budge from his spot. "Five kids, huh? I have three myself. They're all grown, of course, but I wouldn't mind having a few little ones around even at my age. My wife died a few years back, so that's not likely."

"I'm sorry," Maggie said. And she was. There was a sadness lurking in his eyes. She sensed Mort Holmes was a lonely man.

"I live with my mother now," he said. "I figured there was no sense staying in a big house all by myself. Know what I mean?" He smiled. "So what do you do for fun, Maggie?"

"Fun?" She laughed. "There's not much time for that these days," she said, wanting to discourage him from suggesting they should plan to enjoy something fun together if, in fact, that's where he was leading. "Most of my time is spent running children to soccer practice, dance class, and gymnastics."

"My kids were involved in sports too," Mort said. He paused and reached for his wallet. "I have pictures."

"Pictures, huh?" Maggie smiled weakly. It was going to be a long evening. Where the heck was Jason!

"I carry them with me everywhere," Mort told her. "I have more in the car." He opened his battered wallet and leafed through the photos of his children, ranging from kindergarten through college age. Each picture had a story, Maggie discovered. A long-drawn-out story. She was over- whelmingly thankful when she looked up and found Jason standing in the doorway, holding several bags of ice and grinning at her for all he was worth.

"Maggie, glad you could make it. I see you've met Mort."

Maggie forced herself to smile as Jason wedged himself between her and the other man and dumped the bags of ice in the sink. His denim- clad thigh brushed against hers and sent a flash of heat up to her hipbone. She was reminded once again of that kiss. Reminded, hell, she thought. She hadn't stopped thinking about the kiss long enough to be *reminded* of it. She opened her mouth to speak, but Mort beat her to it.

"Yes, Maggie and I are getting along wonderfully," he said, smiling at her as though they were old friends. He winked at her and drained his glass. "Say, Maggie, I'm starved. Can I get you something from the buffet?"

She nodded enthusiastically, hoping to snatch a moment alone with Jason. "That would be great."

She didn't waste any time once Mort had disappeared into the next room. "Jason, what's going on?" she demanded.

He glanced up from the sink, where he'd just torn open one of the bags of ice and was in the process of filling an ice bucket. "What do you mean?"

"Why is that man sticking to me like chewing gum? And why do I have the strangest suspicion I'm supposed to be his *date* for the evening?" She somehow managed to make the word *date* sound like one of those four-letter words found on public bathroom walls.

Jason looked surprised. "What's wrong with Mort?" he said. "I sort of figured the two of you would hit it off. He's very *mature* and *responsible*, you know. And did I mention he's an accountant? You know how *trustworthy* and *dependable* accountants are."

"I don't care if he's a Baptist minister," she said. "I don't want you fixing me up with him or anybody else. I can find my *own* dates, thank you very much." It had never occurred to her that Jason would do such a thing. Nor had it occurred to her how hurt she would be because of it.

"Hey, what are friends for?"

"You're just trying to get back at me for the other night."

This time Jason looked hurt. "On the contrary, darlin'. I'm only trying to give you what you asked for. You said you wanted an older man who wouldn't be afraid of responsibility. I immediately thought of ol' Mort." He grinned. "He lives with his mother, you know. She's eighty-eight, and she still packs his lunch for him every day. Guess what he eats?"

His blue eyes were bright with amusement. No man had a right to look that good, Maggie told herself. "I wouldn't know," she said.

"Tuna fish on whole wheat." His grin broadened. "Day after day after day."

That smile would have melted glaciers. It was already turning her knees to mush. Her toes tingled. She wondered if he had any idea what that smile did to women. "So what?"

He stepped closer, backing her against the opposite cabinet. She knew he was purposely trying to get her all flustered, and she wasn't about to let him know he'd succeeded. He certainly was going to a lot of trouble to find all her buttons and push them. He didn't stop until his thighs were pressed flush against hers, until she had a sense of hard, tight muscle, until she felt her heart land in the back of her throat. His breath was warm on her face when he spoke, and Maggie realized she was holding her own breath. It gushed out when she released it. "Is that what you want from a man, Maggie?" he whispered. "Are you willing to settle for a tuna-fish sort of guy when you could have a chili cheeseburger with all the trimmings?"

Maggie refused to meet his gaze. Instead, she fastened her eyes on his chest, where his shirt collar fell open slightly and exposed just enough chest hair to intrigue. "You're not making any sense, Jason," she said. "Did you drop one of those bags of ice on your head? Or maybe Billy-Bob hit you harder than we thought the other night, and you're suffering a delayed reaction."

He was prevented from answering when Mort spoke from the doorway. "Here we are, Maggie," he said. "I didn't know what you liked, so I got you one of everything. Hope you're hungry."

Maggie stepped from between Jason and the cabinet and reached for the paper plate filled with snacks and finger sandwiches. "Thank you, Mort," she said, her cheeks flaming from embarrassment. Why did she allow Jason to do these things to her? "It looks delicious." She was glancing at the food as she said it, but she was thinking of Jason's mouth and that kiss. She'd heard it said before that the flesh was weak, but she was downright pitiful where Jason Profitt was concerned.

"Everybody from the office chipped in and brought something," Mort said. "Mother and I made sandwiches. Do you like tuna fish?"

Maggie offered him a vague smile as Jason chuckled from behind.

Three nights later Maggie pulled Jason aside at soccer practice. "Call him off," she demanded.

"Who?"

"You know darn good and well who."

"What's wrong, Maggie darlin'?"

It was hard to concentrate on being mad at a man who looked so good in denim, who smelled like something out of a fantasy. "I'll tell you what's wrong. Your friend, Mort Holmes, is driving me crazy! He has called me every day since the party.

Not only that, he's sending flowers. My house smells like a funeral parlor."

Jason chuckled. "*My* friend? I thought Mort was *your* friend."

"That's not funny."

He tried to look serious, but his blue eyes were bright with laughter. "Look, Maggie, you told me—"

"I don't care *what* I told you. I don't want that man calling me anymore. Now, what are you going to do about it?"

"Me?" His gaze dropped briefly to her breasts, and he was reminded of the things he liked best about her. He was glad she didn't diet herself into a beanpole figure like some of the women he'd known who were more concerned with looking chic than how they felt in a man's arms. She was soft and curvy and more feminine than any woman he'd ever met. And that spelled sexy in his mind. "You're a big girl," he said, raising his eyes to her face. "*You* tell him."

Maggie blushed, feeling as though Jason had actually caressed her breasts with his hands. All at once she felt warm and tingly. She folded her arms over her chest and tried to act casual, but she knew she would never be able to pull it off. Jason knew exactly the kind of effect he was having on her. And here she was supposed to be a woman without passion. "I don't want to hurt Mort's feelings," she said after a moment.

"But you don't have a problem hurting mine, right?" It annoyed him that she could be so concerned over another man's feelings when she didn't have a problem in the world telling *him* where to get off.

"That's different. You can take care of yourself. Besides, I sort of feel sorry for Mort."

Jason sighed. "Okay, I'll talk to him," he said

begrudgingly. "But it's not going to be easy. The guy is wild for you, Maggie darlin'. He may look tame on the outside, but underneath it all he's hotter than a firecracker."

She rolled her eyes heavenward. "Give me a break." She turned to leave, then paused. "And one other thing. Stop calling me darling. People might think—" She started to say something, then thought better of it.

"What might people think, Maggie? That we're lovers?"

She raised her head, and their gazes collided. The look she saw in his eyes made her heart beat a little faster. Jason Profitt desired her. It was written all over his handsome face. Once again she felt that old familiar pull, as though he were slowly reeling her in on an invisible line. If she had not known he wanted her in his bed before, she knew it without a doubt now. And that left her as frightened and confused as a skater on thin ice. "Uh, never mind," she mumbled after a moment, and hurried away.

The following night Maggie pounded on Jason's door. He smiled the minute he opened it. "Maggie darlin'. I didn't know you were dropping by. You're just in time for supper."

The speech she'd been practicing on the way over lodged in the back of her throat when she caught sight of his devilish grin and boyishly tousled hair. What was it about the man that always made her pulse race and thoughts scatter like tumbleweed in a dust storm.

"I won't be staying," she said, shoving past him and his after-shave with a large pot of chrysanthemums in her arms. She set it down on his coffee table with a loud thud.

"There's more in the car," she said, indicating the pot before disappearing through the door. She returned with a vase of long-stemmed roses and a basket of daisies. "I can't keep them at my place because Molly has allergies."

"Where in the world did you get all these flowers?" Jason asked once she carried in a final load of day lilies and carnations.

"Take a wild guess." Maggie crossed her arms and regarded the man, fixing her gaze on his wide chest so that she wasn't forced to notice with mouth-watering clarity how those low-riding denims hugged his hips and thighs. "I thought you were going to call him off."

"You mean Mort?" Jason shook his head as though truly vexed. "I tried, Maggie, but the guy won't listen. I'm telling you, he's got it bad."

"No man would send all these flowers unless he was being encouraged."

"Then cut it out."

Her face flamed. "I'm not doing anything!"

He was the picture of innocence, but his eyes were bright with humor. "You don't think I—"

"What did you tell him about me, Jason?"

He shrugged. "Just that you'd been divorced awhile."

"Did you imply that maybe I was *lonely* and *needed* a man in my life? That I was *desperate* for love? That I was no longer able to *contain* my *desires*?"

Now he looked hurt. "Of course not. What d'you think I am?"

She paused. "I'd rather not answer that at the moment. I thought you were my friend. Thanks to you, I've got some weirdo calling all hours of the day and night." She continued to scold him, telling him how Mort had interrupted an important business meeting at work that day with one of his calls. Finally, she was forced to stop and draw in a fresh breath. She sniffed. "Is something burning?"

"My dinner!" Jason raced to the kitchen with Maggie at his heels. He reached for the metal handle on the skillet. It was hot as a poker. "Ouch, damn!" He released it, almost knocking it off the stove in the process.

"Here, let me do it," Maggie said, worried that he may have burned himself badly. She slipped between him and the stove, grabbed an oven mitt, and moved the skillet from the hot burner. "Are you okay?" she asked once she'd turned the stove off.

Jason was sucking on his finger. "Yeah, I'm fine," he mumbled. "But I don't think I can say the same for my dinner," he added when she lifted the lid from the pan. Steam and smoke forced them back.

Maggie reached over the stove and flipped on the exhaust fan. "Why didn't you tell me you had something cooking?"

"You never gave me a chance."

"What's this supposed to be anyway?" she asked, taking a closer look at the charred dish.

"Beef Stroganoff. What does it look like?"

"Never mind. Maybe you can still save some of it." But her tone was doubtful. Then she remembered his hand. "Do you want me to put something on that burn?"

"Your lips, if it's not too much trouble."

She resisted the urge to smile. "Sorry. The only booboos I kiss are those belonging to my children."

Jason was prevented from coaxing her further into a little TLC when the phone rang. He picked it up, then grinned when the party spoke from the other end. "Oh, hello, Mort," he said, and was rewarded with a dark look from Maggie. He listened for a moment. "Did you try to reach her at home?"

Maggie knew from the smile on Jason's face that they were discussing her. "Tell him," she whispered, "or you'll be *wearing* the Stroganoff."

Jason's grin broadened. "Uh, listen, Mort, maybe you should back off. I don't think Maggie is interested in a relationship right now." He paused. "Yeah, I know you're crazy about her. She likes you too, but she doesn't have much time for romance these days. I knew you'd understand, Mort." Finally, he hung up. "Okay, it's taken care of."

Maggie sighed her relief. "Thank you."

"But it's too late for him to stop the ficus tree from being delivered tomorrow."

"Ficus tree?"

"You should have told me you had this kind of effect on men, Maggie darlin'." He stepped close.

The kitchen suddenly shrank in size, and Maggie was immediately very much aware of his closeness. Every nerve in her body snapped to attention. "Don't be ridiculous," she said in a matter-of-fact tone that didn't even hint at the discomfort she was feeling. She couldn't be in the same room with him without wanting to stand closer. And she couldn't stand close to him without wanting to touch him, even in some small way.

Jason shook his head sadly. "Oh, Maggie. You don't know your own power." He stepped closer, until the front of his thighs touched hers. His eyes caressed her lips before they met her own gaze.

"Now that we've gotten Mort out of the way, can we stop playing games?"

The huskiness in his voice made her toes curl. Maggie tilted her head back. She felt dazed. A sweet lethargy fell over her as he continued to look at her, his eyes warming the dark corners of her heart, that part of her that had forgotten what it was like to be attracted to a man. One gold curl fell across his forehead, and she was tempted to brush it away. But she didn't because she was half afraid it wouldn't be enough, and she'd end up in his arms again, her fingers plunged into his golden mane. "What games?" she asked after a moment.

Jason would have given anything to know what she was thinking, what had put that flush on her face, that look of vulnerability in her eyes. He wanted to take her in his arms. "You're not interested in a man like Mort Holmes. You're still young and pretty, Maggie, with your whole life ahead of you. Don't set your sights on an older man who has already lived much of his life and is ready to retire."

"What do I need with a younger man?" she asked, knowing exactly where the conversation was going.

"Three years is nothing."

"Three years and five children."

"Why won't you take a chance on me?" When she looked away, Jason slipped his arms around her waist and pulled her closer. "Why won't you take a chance on *us*?"

Finally, she looked at him. "You were right about me, Jason," she said. "I'm scared. Not only for my children, but for myself. I was devastated when my ex-husband left. I felt like such a failure." She shook her head sadly. "As a wife and mother, and as a woman."

"Did it ever occur to you that you were married to a jerk?" he asked. "Why is it important to you to shoulder all the blame for what happened?"

"Why are *you* so intent on defending me?" she said. "You don't know me."

"I know you better than you think, Maggie darlin'. And I'm tired of watching you beat up on yourself." He kissed the tip of her nose. "Look, I'm not going to make any promises I can't keep, but I want to continue seeing you. And I don't want you setting a bunch of limits for me. I don't want you to keep me away from your children or things that are important to you. Say you'll give it a chance, Maggie. Let me come into your life." He grinned, but she didn't look any closer to giving in than she had when she'd walked through that door. Patience. That's what he needed. Patience and a lot of firm self-control and cold showers. "At least let me come home with you for dinner," he said, deciding it was best not to push her when she wasn't quite ready. He could be as cool as the next guy if he had to.

But only for a little while longer.

Maggie gazed up at him, knowing she didn't have the heart to say no when she was responsible for his burnt meal. Besides, the children were out with Bob, and the thought of eating alone depressed her. "I suppose the least I can do is feed you," she said, knowing he had somehow wheedled his way into spending another evening with her. Despite her better judgment, she wanted to be with him too. "But I'm not promising anything more than that," she said, wondering if she was trying to convince him or herself.

Five

"Where is everybody?" Jason asked the minute he followed Maggie into her house twenty minutes later. There wasn't a child in sight.

"Bob took the kids out for hamburgers." She chuckled. "Don't worry, they won't be gone long." She motioned him to follow her into the kitchen. "I hope you like chicken and broccoli casserole," she said hopefully.

"Sounds great. What can I do to help?"

Maggie pulled a baking dish from the refrigerator and unwrapped it. "You can set the table if you like," she said, surprised that he was so eager to help. "I just have to pop this in the microwave to warm up."

They chatted about the progress Davey was making in soccer while Jason set the kitchen table and Maggie prepared a small tossed salad to go with the casserole. Once they sat down, she glanced around the room, half expecting to find a child lurking in the corner. "I don't know if I can eat with all this silence," she confessed.

He reached for her hand and squeezed it. "I don't know how you do it, Maggie."

She chuckled. "Sometimes not very well."

He tasted his salad. "You do a great job of taking care of everybody else. I wish you'd take as good care of yourself."

His words surprised her and made her feel defensive at the same time. Even though she sometimes felt overwhelmed with all her responsibilities, she had never regretted having as many children as she did. "I do nice things for myself," she said after a moment.

"Like what?"

She thought about it. "Well, sometimes when everybody's asleep, I run a hot bath and grab a good book and relax for an hour. I know I need to take time for myself."

"Don't you ever resent being the caretaker of so many people?"

She didn't answer right away. She had never been one to whine and complain, and with the exception of Cynthia, kept her feelings and frustrations to herself. But this was Jason, and she knew instinctively she could trust him as much as she did her best friend. "I suppose I resent Bob," she said at last. "My children didn't *ask* to be born. But now that they're here, they need love and attention. I suppose I begrudge the fact that some men can walk away from a family without giving it a second thought. I wouldn't think of abandoning my children."

"Not all men are like that."

She thought of the other women she knew who were struggling to raise children without the benefit of a husband. There was never enough money, even for those women fortunate enough to receive reliable child support payments, which she did not. She could always drag her ex-husband back into court, of course, and protest his sporadic payments. *If* she didn't mind forking out money to her attorney and missing work to appear before the judge. But she didn't tell Jason all that because, once again, she didn't want to sound like a complainer. Somehow, she would make it. She always did.

"I know there are good men in this world," she told him. Then, with a chuckle, she added, "Unfortunately, I didn't marry one of them. But that's okay. My children are healthy and well-adjusted and we haven't had to go hungry. Every time I start feeling overwhelmed or sorry for myself, I turn on the news and discover that I'm actually very lucky."

He studied her. "I envy you, Maggie."

She laughed. "Me? Why on earth would *you* envy *me*?" She thought of his posh, uncluttered apartment with its new furniture, while her own stuff was literally falling apart.

"It feels good here," he said, glancing around the kitchen with its old-fashioned print wallpaper. "Warm and cozy. Like a real home. My place feels like a hotel room."

She laughed. "But your place is quiet," she pointed out. "It's *never* quiet here." She shook her head. "With all the bickering that goes on, you can't even hear yourself think. I guess that's the way it is with brothers and sisters, though." She was suddenly curious about him. "Do you come from a large family?"

He shook his head. "I was an only child."

"Davey wants to be an only child," she said.

"It's not that great, believe me. I would've given anything to have a brother or sister."

"What are your parents like?"

He thought about it. "I could never figure out why they were together," he said. "I mean, they were so different from each other. Still are."

She smiled. "They say opposites attract."

"Not in this case, I'm afraid. My parents haven't shared a bedroom in years." It startled him when he realized what he'd said.

"Is something wrong?" Maggie asked, noting the pensive look in those blue eyes.

"I've never told anybody that. About my parents, I mean."

"I won't repeat it."

"I know." He reached for her hand and squeezed it. He knew his secrets were safe with her. "It's just—" He paused. "I haven't wanted to admit it to myself, but I don't think they've been in love for years."

"What makes you say that?"

"They don't smile at each other. There's no warmth between them."

"Do they argue a lot?"

He shook his head. "Never. That's the point. If they were fighting, I'd think there was still some spark left." He took a bite of his casserole and chewed thoughtfully. "That's one reason I was never in a hurry to marry. I assumed all marriages were like that."

"Do you still feel that way?"

"No."

"What changed your mind?"

"Well, until recently, most of my friends were single. But my new boss had me over to dinner a couple of times, and I have to tell you, I really enjoy spending time with him and his wife. They've been married eighteen years, and it's obvious they're still very much in love. They work at it, though. He still calls her once or twice a day. She sends goofy little cards." He smiled. "I couldn't imagine her moving into the spare bedroom." This time he laughed. "I couldn't imagine my boss allowing it."

"What would you do?"

"You mean if I were married and my wife decided to move into the spare bedroom?" He thought about it. "Well, first I'd kick my own butt for not noticing there was a problem. Then I'd probably resort to caveman tactics."

Her fork poised in midair, Maggie looked up in surprise. "Like what?"

"I'd haul her fanny right back in there, and I wouldn't let her out until we fixed the problem." He grinned. "Then I'd make love to her so good that she wouldn't *ever* think of doing it again. You see, I'm a firm believer that a husband and wife should share the same bed."

For a moment all Maggie could do was stare at the look of naked aggression in his eyes. Something in his look told her that while Jason might be willing to give and take in other areas of a relationship, he would expect total surrender between the sheets. At the same time, she could not imagine a woman choosing not to share a bed with him. She knew he would be a wonderful lover. He was sensitive and caring enough that he would spend as much time as he needed to prepare a woman for lovemaking, and he had enough male ego about him that he would see her satisfied. She saw the generous, giving side of him when he dealt with her children, especially Davey, encouraging him, making him believe in himself as his own parents had never been able to do. She felt the sensual, masculine side of him every time she turned and caught him watching her, each time he brushed past her or looked into her eyes.

They ate for a moment in silence, each of them aware of the sudden tension that had sprung up between them. Maggie felt flushed and self-conscious. Her fork clanged loudly on the plate when she set it down, causing them both to jump.

"Sorry." She laughed and reached for her iced tea, wishing she could raise it to her warm face.

"Maybe they felt they had to stay together," Jason said after a moment.

"Who?" Maggie's face went blank.

"My parents."

Maggie blushed, realizing she had somehow dropped the thread of their conversation. "Oh, yes, your parents."

"They've been through a lot, financially speaking. They started out with nothing, and now—" He paused, thinking of the hardships his parents had lived through in their early days, in what his father jokingly referred to as their pre-Mercedes days. "Now they have everything except what's important."

Maggie thought he looked sad. "Maybe they're staying together for other reasons."

"What do you mean?"

"Sometimes people stay together because it feels comfortable. For some people that's as important as having stars in your eyes and butterflies in your stomach."

"Is that why you stayed with Bob?"

This time Maggie dropped her fork. It clattered against her plate. She started to pick it up, then changed her mind and reached for her glass instead. "I thought we were talking about your parents."

"You're a cool card, Maggie," he said. "You don't give anything away, do you?"

She grinned. "Not if I can help it."

He leaned close. "One day you'll open up to me," he said. "In more ways than one."

Maggie shifted uneasily in her chair as he continued to watch her, his blue eyes taking on an almost feral expression. Finally, he turned his attention back to his meal, and she was able to relax a bit. She thought about what he'd said about his parents, and she was reminded once again how different their backgrounds were. Jason had obviously come from money while, after the death of her father, her family had lived in near poverty.

Maggie couldn't relate to a man who'd attended boarding schools and lived in a place like West Palm Beach. She already knew he had graduated from one of the best engineering schools in the country. She and her sister had barely managed to graduate high school. They hadn't gone off to college like their friends. There simply hadn't been any money and, besides, they'd had to work full-time. Maggie felt the gulf widen between her and Jason.

"What does your father do?" she asked after a moment.

"He used to sell real estate. He started out in residential, then moved to commercial. He did very well for himself. So well he was able to retire at fifty. Now he spends a lot of time fishing."

"And your mother?"

He shrugged. "She lives for the beauty parlor and lunch with friends."

"What's she like?"

Jason thought about it. "A woman who craves constant order." He chuckled. "She doesn't like noise because she's prone to migraines, and she would never consider having a pet in the house because she's allergic to all fur except gray fox and mink."

Maggie rolled her eyes. "She wouldn't last five minutes in this place."

Jason suspected she was right. "Maybe that's why I like it here so much."

Maggie was about to respond, when the front door was suddenly flung open by five-year-old Molly. "They're back," she said. "So much for a quiet meal."

"It just proves we have to appreciate the time we *do* have alone," he told her.

Maggie was both touched and surprised that Jason could be so understanding. Most men would have been thoroughly annoyed by the sudden arrival of a woman's ex-husband and five children. She pushed her chair from the table and rose to leave just as Davey rushed into the room, grinning from ear to ear, thoroughly delighted that his coach had decided to visit him.

On Friday Maggie was about to start dinner, when the doorbell rang. She opened the door and found Jason standing on the other side, holding two large pizza boxes. The twins spotted him from the living room and came running. "What are you doing here?" Maggie asked.

He stepped through the doorway. "Didn't Jessie tell you I was springing for dinner tonight? I decided we should celebrate how well we did in our first game Wednesday."

"We lost that game, Jason."

"But we played hard, and that's what counts. And Davey proved to be a very promising goalie."

That was stretching the truth a bit, Maggie knew. Davey still had his work cut out for him where soccer was concerned. Still, she was thankful for Jason's optimism. "You're sweet for doing this," she said, motioning for him to follow her into the kitchen. "And no, Jessie didn't tell me you were coming. She's been on the phone since before I walked through the door."

Jason set the boxes on the kitchen table. "You haven't cooked yet, have you?" he asked, glancing at the stove, where a pack of unopened hamburger meat rested beside a skillet.

"I was just about to start."

"Great, now you don't have to. Does everybody like pepperoni and cheese? I decided to order simple toppings, since I don't know who eats what."

"Perfect," she said, glad that he had ordered something her children would eat and she would not have to spend the evening picking off black olives and mushrooms and a bunch of other unwelcome ingredients. The twins seconded her opinion, and Davey was thrilled that it was to be his celebration dinner. While Maggie went about setting the table, Molly did her level best to open one of the boxes. Chuckling to himself, Jason put a piece of pizza on the child's plate so she could go ahead and eat.

"You're very popular around here at the moment," Maggie told Jason once they'd all sat down to dinner. "My children are crazy about Italian food."

"How about their mother? What does she like?"

Maggie grinned. "She likes not having to cook."

Once they'd eaten every last piece of pizza, Jason told Maggie to relax on the sofa while he and the kids cleaned up. They were only too happy to oblige when he told them he had a new Disney video in the car, but Maggie insisted they all put on their pajamas before settling down in front of the television. "Why don't you and I sit on the porch?" he suggested to Maggie. "The movie ought to keep 'em still for a while." Glad to snatch a moment alone with him, she grabbed a sweater from the hall closet and followed him out.

"Jason, why are you doing all this?" Maggie asked once they were alone on the front porch swing. The night was cool and star-filled. "I mean, I appreciate it, but I would think a single guy like you would have more interesting things to do than spend a Friday night with a woman and her five children. I just don't get it."

He looked surprised. "I'm enjoying myself, Maggie. Aren't you?"

"Yes, but—"

"And I like you. I like you so much that it really doesn't matter what we do as long as we spend time together. And if I can make things a little easier for you when I'm around—" He shrugged. "What's wrong with that?"

She glanced away, simply because it was so hard to think straight when he was sitting close to her, when she had to inhale his after-shave every time she took a breath, when she was forced to look into those gorgeous eyes. "I suppose it's okay once in a while." But she wasn't so sure. She was afraid to start counting on him, afraid to let her guard down for one instant and find herself needing him. Every time she had ever needed anyone, she'd gotten hurt.

Jason didn't miss the wariness in her eyes before she turned away from him. He wondered what had put it there all of a sudden. Until that moment, everything had been fine. He wondered if it had anything to do with the fact they were alone. As long as the children were around and things were hectic, Maggie didn't seem to mind having him around. But the minute it got quiet, she backed off. He wondered if she realized she was trying to hide behind her children.

"Maggie?"

"Yes?"

He heard the anxiety in her voice. She was worried about something, and he couldn't imagine what it was. Could it be that she didn't appreciate his dropping by as he had? Had he threatened her sense of independence by doing so? Or did she think he expected a little bit of necking on her front porch now that he'd fed her children? Jason couldn't figure it. Obviously, she wasn't accustomed to people doing nice things for her, and it was even more obvious she didn't want to sit in the dark with him. Was she afraid she would end up in his arms again if she stayed out there for very long? Could she sense how desperately he *wanted* to hold her? It was getting so he couldn't be in the same room with her without thinking of that kiss, without wanting to crush her in his arms and taste her again.

"I'd better go," he said abruptly.

Maggie glanced up in surprise. "So soon?"

He thought he saw disappointment in her eyes. Well, what the hell did she expect from him? He couldn't be expected to just sit there like an old friend and talk superficial nonsense when there was so much more he wanted to say. And do. He obviously wanted more than she was willing to give at the moment, both emotionally *and* physically. Which meant he simply would have to be patient. Again.

Jason stood. "Yeah, it's getting late."

Maggie stood as well, then wished she hadn't when she found herself face-to-face with him and much too close for comfort. She tried to take a step back but felt the porch swing at the backs of her thighs. With no place to go, she clasped her hands together in front of her and regarded him, meeting his steady gaze with one of her own.

"Well, thanks for everything," she said, a bit breathless as she studied his face in the semi-darkness. There was something quite magnificent and incredible about Jason Profitt's face in the dappled moonlight, she decided. She knew he wanted to kiss her. The look in his eyes said it all. For a brief moment she wanted to be whisked away to that place where only Jason could take her. In his arms she could forget her duties and responsibilities and all the things she had to do before she climbed into bed that night.

Jason touched her cheek with the tips of his fingers. For once Maggie didn't freeze on him. The soft, yielding look in her eyes told him that she wanted him to kiss her. She was an odd creature, he decided. When pursued, she ran in the opposite direction. But the moment he retreated, she suddenly seemed interested. What man could figure the inner workings of a woman? he thought. At the same time, he decided it might be wise to back off and see where it took them. He wasn't getting anywhere with her the other way.

"Good night, Maggie," he said, and this time he was certain of the disappointment in her eyes. It pleased him that he'd been able to discover some integral part of her personality. He shoved his hands deep into his pockets, turned, and made his way to his car. He felt more cocky and self-assured than he had in days now that he'd figured her out, and there was a bounce in his step as he crossed her front yard.

Maggie was clearly puzzled as she watched

Jason climb into his car and drive away. If she lived to be a hundred and ten, she would never be able to figure out what went on in a man's head. Just when she'd been willing to let Jason sweep her off her feet, he'd turned and gone in the opposite direction, and she was left with a sense of loneliness and yearning she hadn't felt in a long time.

What was a woman to do?

Maggie was ironing the following evening when Jason called. "What'd you do today?" he asked.

She smiled, her heart aflutter at the sound of his voice. She had thought about him all day and wondered why he'd left so abruptly the night before without a kiss. "Well, after soccer practice I ran errands and did a few chores around the house."

"Hmmm. Sounds like you need a treat. Why don't we all go out for ice cream?"

"I can't. Molly's already in bed."

"Okay, then, why don't I bring the ice cream to you?"

She glanced around the cluttered living room, where Davey and the twins were watching a television show. Jessie was cleaning out her school notebook, and the mountain of wadded paper confirmed the fact that it had been a while since the last time she'd done so. Although Maggie had tidied the place that morning, it hadn't stayed that way long. Next to her, though, the house looked great. She'd been so busy with everything else that she hadn't had time to do anything to herself. It was more than apparent in her unmade-up face and sloppy sweats. Still, this was the *real* Maggie Farnsworth, she told herself, the woman who seldom found time for manicures and facials and bubble baths. Perhaps it was time Jason saw how unglamorous her life really was.

"Okay," she said after a moment. "We'll be here."

"Great. What flavor should I get?"

"Surprise us."

When Maggie let Jason in the front door thirty minutes later, she had at least run a comb through her hair, brushed her teeth, and applied lipstick. If he thought she looked bad without makeup, he didn't say anything.

"I didn't know what you guys liked, so I bought several different flavors," he said, setting down a large sack. He pulled out three half-gallon cartons. "There's butter pecan, chocolate fudge, and French vanilla."

Maggie chuckled. "You're crazy, you know that?"

"Crazy about you." He leaned forward and kissed her pert nose, although the desire to kiss her full on the lips was strong.

They ate their ice cream at the kitchen table, but Maggie allowed Jessie and Davey to eat on the floor in front of the television set. "You know, you don't have to buy food every time you want to visit," Maggie told him once she'd polished off her bowl of butter pecan. "You're going to spoil me."

He took her hand and squeezed it, then held it for a moment, studying her green eyes. The twins had gone back into the living room, giving them a little privacy. "What's wrong with that?" He tried to make his voice sound light, but it was a question he desperately wanted answered.

Lord, but he was gorgeous when he looked at her that way. Maggie shifted in her chair as he continued his perusal. She wondered if he had any idea what he did to women when he smiled that sexy half-smile of his. She regretted now that she hadn't at least brushed on a little blush. Then she realized he was waiting for her to answer. She shrugged. "Nothing, I suppose. I just don't want to get used to it." She regretted it the minute she said it.

"In case I stop coming around?" He smiled gently. So that was it. "Is that what you're afraid of, Maggie?"

"Maybe." She saw the thoughtful look on his face. "I don't mean to sound ungrateful," she said. "I mean, you're such a nice guy and all." She sighed.

Jason released her hand. He didn't say anything right away, simply because he was so irritated. If she referred to him as a nice guy once more, he was going to put her over his knee. He wasn't so nice, he wanted to tell her. If she had any idea of the fantasies he'd had of her lately, she'd grab her children and run as fast as she could in the opposite direction. Which was why he didn't tell her. He didn't want to put that wary look on her face once more.

"Why don't you and I take a walk?" he said instead, hoping the fresh air would clear his head and ease the sudden tension that had sprung up between them. He saw it in her face—the heightened color, the way she didn't quite meet his gaze. As long as they were occupied, busily doing something physical or something that required concentration, they didn't have time to sit around and think about each other. He didn't have to sit there and think about what he would *like* to be doing to her. "We don't have to go far," he added. "Just around the block. It's nice out."

It sounded good to someone who'd spent the day inside cleaning. Besides, it was getting too quiet between them, Maggie told herself. Strained. She could feel the tension in the air each time his eyes found her lips and lingered there. "Okay." She carried their bowls to the sink and went for her sweater, giving brief orders to her children.

The night air was cool and crisp as they stepped out onto the front porch. Jason linked his fingers with Maggie's and led her down the steps and across the front yard to the cracked sidewalk. He took a moment to study the neighborhood. It was older. Established. There was a feeling of permanence about the place. Stability. He saw it in the gnarled oaks that flanked the narrow street, the tall, red-tipped privacy hedges that separated driveways and yards.

How different from his own upbringing in fancy high-rise apartments. After an early retirement, his father had purchased a luxury ocean-front condominium in a trendy section of West Palm Beach, where he now spent much of his time on his new fishing boat. It wasn't until Jason had begun engineering school that the two had grown close. Jared Profitt simply hadn't had time for his son until then. Jason regretted all the years they'd missed.

"How long have you lived here?" he asked Maggie after they had walked a short distance.

"Three years." Maggie couldn't help but wonder what he thought of the area with its compact houses shoved so close together. Many of her neighbors were older and retired and living on fixed incomes. Nevertheless they took pride in their homes. The grass was always neatly trimmed, the walks free of clutter, and the trim around the windows painted the moment the color began to fade. Yet it was uncomfortably close to the downtown area, where neighborhoods were falling into disrepair and succumbing to crime. The previous month the police had raided a crack house only six blocks away. More and more Maggie was beginning to feel time was running out for her and her children. But where else could she go? She barely made ends meet as it was.

"Bob and I owned a nicer place north of here," she said after a moment, "but I couldn't keep up the payments after the divorce." She said it matter-of-factly and without a hint of self-pity. She wouldn't tell him how she had worked weekends in a real estate office to try to make the mortgage or how her children had suffered in the meantime because they seldom saw her. In the end she had sold it for less than it was worth so she could get out from under the payments. It had taken almost every dime she'd had to pay the deposits on the new house and get them moved. Bob hadn't so much as offered to assist.

"Your ex-husband helps you, doesn't he?" Jason asked as though reading her mind.

"I can't always count on it."

"Have you said anything to him?" He was prying, but he couldn't help it.

"It doesn't do any good. The only way I'm going to get Bob's attention is take him back to court. But that's expensive and takes time."

"It might be worth it in the long run, though." She shrugged, and Jason got the impression she really didn't care to discuss it. He could tell she was a proud woman, a woman who wouldn't want to confess her financial problems to anyone. He could see it in the determined tilt of her chin, the stubborn look in her eyes. He wondered what it would take to break down that tough exterior of hers, the concrete wall that surrounded her. He knew her children were capable of getting through;

he'd seen it enough. He wasn't so sure she would ever let another man in.

They circled the block, holding hands like youngsters while Maggie told him a little about her neighbors. At the same time, she seemed to hurry.

"I'm sorry if I seem rushed," she said, "but I still have a lot of ironing to do."

"Why don't you do some of it tomorrow?"

"That's the day I buy groceries, plan meals for the week, and make sure everything is ready for Monday morning."

He chuckled. "What would happen if you let it slide once in a while?"

"Let it slide?" She looked at him. "You mean *not* do it?" She saw that he looked amused. He probably was. But then, how could she expect him, a confirmed bachelor, to understand what she had to do in order for her life to run smoothly? "I've let it slide once or twice before," she said. "Believe me, it's not a pretty sight."

They had reached her house. "Okay, I'll go so you can get back to your chores," he told her, his tone reluctant. He wanted to keep on talking to her, walking with her, holding her hand.

"Well, thanks for the ice cream," Maggie said. She started to walk away.

Jason reached for her hand. "Maggie, wait." He smiled when she glanced up in question. "When can I see you again?"

She shrugged. "Come by anytime," she said. "I'm usually home when I'm not working."

"No, I don't mean that way," he said.

"You could drop by for coffee after the soccer game next week," she suggested.

And Jason knew that he would be counting the hours until then. "I'll call you."

"Okay." She started to walk away once again.

"Uh, Maggie?"

"Is there something else?"

He nodded, his former resolve forgotten. He wanted to kiss her, dammit, and that's exactly what he was going to do. "Just this," he said, and lowered his head.

Before she knew what was happening, Jason was kissing her. His touch was warm and tasted sweet from the ice cream he'd eaten earlier. The kiss was slow and unhurried, one that conveyed friendship and simple caring. Maggie relaxed against him. It seemed only natural when he parted her lips with his tongue. He slid it back and forth across her full bottom lip but never rushed in despite the fact that Maggie would have gladly welcomed it. He was obviously taking his time with her, and that made her all the more anxious, made her want it all the more.

Finally, he released her. "Good night, Maggie darlin'," he said gently.

She watched as he climbed into his car and pulled away, wondering how she would ever make it until the next soccer game. And that thought frightened her. She didn't want to look forward to seeing him again. Already she could feel that sense of breathlessness that always stole over her whenever she saw him or talked with him on the phone.

That wasn't a good sign!

Six

The next few weeks found Davey and Jason practicing soccer almost daily in the backyard. In addition, the team practiced on Saturday morning and played a game on Tuesday night. Although Davey was making progress as the team goalie, Maggie knew there were other boys better suited for the position, and she wondered, deep in her heart, if Jason was keeping Davey in the goalie box because of her. She didn't say anything. Her son was blossoming under Jason's guidance and enthusiasm. Even Cynthia noticed the changes taking place in the boy.

"The child is obviously crazy about the man," Cynthia said at one of the soccer games. "And from those stars in your eyes, I'd say you were too."

Maggie shifted on the bleacher. She really wasn't ready to discuss her feelings about Jason, not even with her best friend.

"We're just friends, Jason and I," she said.

"Yeah, sure you are." When Maggie didn't say anything, Cynthia went on. "This is me, Maggie, your closest friend. I've told you every single secret I've ever had. You *owe* me!"

Maggie sighed heavily. She knew better than to try to hide something from Cynthia. "Okay, I'm crazy about him," she confessed. "He's everything I've ever wanted in a man. He makes me feel—" She paused.

"Yeah?"

"Breathless."

"So what's the problem?"

"I'm scared to death."

A week before Halloween Maggie was at her old sewing machine making costumes: a pirate suit for Davey and a ballerina outfit for Molly. The twins had decided to dress up as Raggedy Ann and Andy. Jessie had announced that she was too old to participate, so that meant one less costume for Maggie to make. She knew she should have her head examined for agreeing to make their costumes instead of buying them at the local department store when she had so many other things to do. But this was one of the things she liked most about having children. She enjoyed every minute of it. Theirs was always the first house on the block to have a pumpkin, and Maggie made sure it was the biggest of the lot. They made a production of carving it—the whole family gathered together for the event. Afterward they made pumpkin bars from the pulp and baked the seeds in the oven. Nothing went to waste.

On Halloween night Maggie was in the process of getting them all in their costumes when Bob called to say he had to work late and couldn't take the kids trick-or-treating. Maggie wasn't surprised, just mad! What *did* surprise her was the fact that he didn't even try to muffle the sound of music in the background. He wasn't at work, she told herself. He was in a bar, probably snuggled up to a size 36D bimbo! When she hung up, she tried her best to look disappointed.

"Daddy can't make it," she said, then felt her heart break at the crestfallen looks on their faces. "He has to work late." She smiled. "But that's okay. I can take you this year."

"Who is going to stay and answer the door?" Davey asked.

Jessie spoke up. "I'll stay. I'm too old for trick-or-treating," she said with a superior air.

"Thanks, Jessie." Maggie smiled at her daughter. "Is everybody ready? Don't forget your sword, Davey." She reached for the sword they'd made out of cardboard and sprayed with silver paint, handed it to her son, and adjusted his black eye-patch. "I must say, you're looking rather ruthless tonight." Except for the caramel-colored freckles spattered across his nose and the missing baby teeth, she thought.

Davey was about to answer, when the doorbell rang. Jessie reached into a large bowl for a treat. "It's only Jason," she said when she opened the door.

"Gee, thanks," he mumbled. "Don't I get a treat?"

"You're not a kid," Jessie told him, putting the miniature candy bar back in the bowl.

"I'm a kid at heart," he said, a grin splitting his handsome face. "Doesn't that count?"

Maggie couldn't get over how glad she was to see him despite his bad timing. "Jason, what are you doing here?"

"I figured you could use a hand tonight," he said, gazing at the excited faces before him. "You guys look great. Let me see if I can guess what you're supposed to be." He pointed to Molly. "Cinderella, right?" When she shook her head, he tried again. "Madonna?"

"No, silly, I'm a ballerina."

"And who are you supposed to be?" he asked Maggie once he'd finished with the others.

She grinned. She wasn't wearing a costume. "I'm the old woman in the shoe."

He nodded, but there was humor in his eyes. "It becomes you."

Maggie smiled back, trying to ignore her fluttering stomach. "And you?" she said, noting his ordinary attire as well. "Who are you posing as tonight?"

"Prince Charming, who else?"

Jessie giggled. "Will you turn into a frog if Mom kisses you?"

Jason would have had to be blind to miss the rosy blush on Maggie's face. He grinned. "I don't know, but I think it's worth the risk."

"Are we going to stand here all night talking about gross things?" Davey demanded, suddenly looking irritated with the whole group. "There won't be any candy left."

"Hold your horses, Blackbeard," Jason told him. "We're right behind you." They filed out the door after the swashbuckling, freckle-faced pirate as Maggie was leaving last-minute instructions for Jessie.

"You're a lifesaver," she told Jason as they waited in front of the house next door while the children scurried up the walk and knocked. "Molly isn't as resilient as her brother and sisters. I'll probably have to take her back early."

Jason watched an elderly woman answer the door and immediately start passing out candy.

"Why didn't you tell me you needed help?" he said. "Or is that too difficult for you to admit?"

Maggie shot him a sidelong glance. "I didn't know I'd need help, smart aleck. Bob had planned to be here."

"And?"

"And he couldn't make it," she responded more sharply than she'd meant to. "Claimed he had to work late."

Jason noted the tense lines near her mouth as they followed the small group of trick-or-treaters to the next house. "And you don't believe him?"

Maggie gave a snort of disgust. "The only kind of business Bob Farnsworth is taking care of tonight is monkey business."

Jason didn't miss the anger in her voice. "Does that upset you?"

"Of course it upsets me. Not because I care what he does. I just don't like to see my children disappointed."

Jason watched the group of laughing youngsters as they held their bags out for a handful of goodies. "They don't look disappointed to me."

"That's because they don't know what a rat their father is. You don't think I told them he'd rather be in some honky-tonk tonight than with them, do you?" She saw that her statement had drawn a frown from him. "I'm sorry," she said. "You shouldn't have to listen to this. I need time to cool off, that's all."

"Why are you protecting him, Maggie?" he asked softly. "Why don't you tell them the truth?"

"I'm not protecting *him*. I'm protecting my children." She huddled more deeply into her sweater. "Let's not talk about it anymore, okay? It upsets me, and I don't want anything to ruin this night for the children."

Jason didn't press her, but he remained thoughtful. It bothered him that Maggie's ex-husband still had the power to bring her to anger. She was never going to be ready for a new relationship if she couldn't let go of the old one.

They had been out only little more than an hour when Molly began to complain about how tired she was. "Go ahead and take her back to the house," Jason said. "I'll take Davey and the twins around."

Maggie was both surprised and delighted. "I'm beginning to think you really are Prince Charming," she said.

"Good. I intend to collect my kiss later," he whispered.

Maggie almost shivered when his warm breath fanned her ear. "Sorry, that's a different fairy tale. Prince Charming and the Frog Prince are two separate stories."

"As long as they have happy endings, that's all that matters. You and I are destined to have a happy ending."

Were they really destined for a happy ending? Maggie wondered. She experienced a moment of giddy anticipation at the thought. Her heart soared. In a voice that gave absolutely nothing away, she said, "I'll see you back at the house in an hour, Kermit."

"With fresh coffee, I hope?"

"Naw, I was going to try to catch a few houseflies in a jar for you." Maggie waved once as she led Molly in the direction of their house.

An hour later Maggie had bathed a sleepy-eyed Molly, straightened the kitchen, and put coffee on, but there was still no sign of Jason and her children.

"I'll bet Davey talked Jason into letting them

stay out later," Jessie said when Maggie checked her watch for the third time.

"You're probably right." Maggie knew her son would try to squeeze every drop of fun he possibly could out of the evening. But when ten o'clock came and went, she decided to go look for them.

"Keep an eye on Molly for me," she told her oldest. "And if Jason gets back before I do, tell him I had to run out for milk."

"You're going looking for him, aren't you?"

Maggie glanced at her as she stuffed her arms into a sweater. "How'd you know?"

"Because there's a whole gallon of milk left in the fridge."

"Do me a favor and don't mention that to Jason." She hurried out the door without another word.

Jason could feel the adrenaline gushing through his body with the force of a fire hose. He and the twins had knocked on every door in the neighborhood, but nobody could recall seeing a red-haired pirate. Don't panic, he told himself. It didn't work. He should *never* have allowed Davey to go down the other side of the street with his friends, even if the boy *had* promised to meet him at the end of the block. Jason had wanted to say no. It was difficult enough to keep up with the twins. But Davey had persisted.

"I hate having to go with my sisters," he'd said. "Everybody will think I'm a sissy. Besides, my dad let me do it last year."

Jason had given in, not only because he didn't want the boy branded a sissy but because he didn't feel justified changing the rules if the boy's father had said it was okay. Another reason, although he hated to admit it, was that he wanted to be accepted and liked by Maggie's children, especially her son, who he suspected needed a friend these days, since his own father appeared too busy for him.

That had been his first mistake, Jason had decided, letting Davey do something so he would like him better. Adults often had to make unpopular decisions to protect children. But that wasn't going to help him now. He needed to act fast!

One of the twins started to cry. Heaven help him, Jason couldn't tell them apart. He knelt in front of the girl, knowing he couldn't feel any worse than he did just then, standing on a sidewalk in the dark, minus one child. A gust of wind flattened her trick-or-treat sack against her legs. "What's wrong, honey?" he asked the girl, wishing Maggie would make the twins wear name tags.

"You lost my brother," the girl said. "I'm never going to see him again."

"It's starting to rain," the other twin said, holding her hand out.

Jason looked up at the sky. A blustery wind whipped across his face, and he felt the first drops of moisture. But of course it would rain, he told himself glumly. He'd been so worried about Davey that he hadn't noticed the change in the weather. He also hadn't noticed they were now the only ones out. The street was bare of trick-or-treaters.

"Let's go back to the house," he said after a long, weary sigh.

"And leave my brother!" the girl cried.

Jason knew he would have preferred crawling on his belly across a bed of hot coals to returning without Maggie's son, but there was nothing else he could do. The rain was beginning to fall harder, and they were at least six blocks from the house. "I'm going to have to go back for my car so I can look for him," Jason told the girl. "It's Amber, isn't it?" he said, knowing he had a fifty percent chance of being right.

"*I'm* Amber," the other girl said. "I know a shortcut home. We'll have to cut through a few backyards, but we can get there in half the time."

"Let's go," Jason said. Just then the sky opened up and drenched them.

The trio looked like wet rats when Jessie let them in ten minutes later. "Where's your mother?" Jason asked, having noticed Maggie's car missing from the driveway.

"Gone for milk," the girl said, averting his gaze.

But Jason knew better. "She's out looking for us, isn't she?"

"I wasn't supposed to tell you. Where's Davey?"

"He lost him," Beth replied with fresh tears.

Jason was about to respond when the phone rang. Jessie grabbed it. "It's Davey," she said.

Jason almost pounced on her. He grabbed the phone. "Davey, where are you?" he demanded, then waited breathlessly for an answer. He hung up a moment later. "Do me a favor, Jessie. Help the girls get into dry clothes while I go for Davey."

"Where is he?"

"A friend's house."

"What do I tell Mom?"

"Don't say anything."

"It won't do any good to try to keep it from her," Jessie told him. "She always finds out sooner or later."

But Jason was already out the door.

• • •

When Maggie walked through the doorway some-time later, she found Jason on the sofa, watching television. She tried not to let her relief show. She had driven up and down every street in the neighborhood, looking for him and her children, but had given up when it began to rain so hard. "Where is everybody?" she asked, having fretted nonstop the past half hour.

Jason yawned, trying his best to act casual despite the fact that he was still unnerved over the events of the night. Although Davey had apologized for not doing as he'd been told, and although Jason had forgiven him, he knew it would be a while before he felt calm again. "Oh, they're in bed," he said. "They promised if I let them stay out later than usual, they would go straight to bed when we got back. Where have *you* been? Don't tell me you were worried about us."

Maggie suddenly felt foolish for driving all over the neighborhood, looking for Jason and her children. He would think she didn't trust him. "No, of course not. I noticed we were low on milk, so I decided to run to the store."

He knew she was fibbing. She was empty-handed, and Jessie had already told him the truth. "So where is it?" he asked, deciding to play along. When her look turned blank, he smiled. "The milk."

Maggie blushed when she realized she had been caught in a bold-faced lie. "Okay, so I *was* worried."

"About what?"

"Well, when you were so late getting back, I was sure something had gone wrong."

Jason was feeling cocky now. He'd managed to fool her after all, despite the fact that Jessie claimed it couldn't be done. He knew Davey would be the last to mention it. "What could go wrong?" he asked. "Don't you think I have enough sense to take three of your children trick-or-treating in their own neighborhood? Gee, Maggie, I don't know what to say." He knew he was pushing it, but he was almost drunk on relief, knowing Davey was now tucked safely in his bed, after he'd spent much of the evening imagining all sorts of terrible things.

Maggie was truly ashamed. "I'm sorry, Jason," she said at last. "I suppose you think I'm overprotective."

Jason pushed himself off the couch and went to her. Perhaps she would feel so guilty over doubting him, she would be more receptive to his advances. Boy, he could be a rat when he wanted. "That's okay, Maggie darlin'. You're not used to trusting people. I understand. But you're going to have to realize you can count on me." He felt like a heel for saying it, especially after he'd spent much of the night looking for the boy he'd lost. But she *did* need to learn to trust again, regardless. And know that she could count on other people, namely him.

Maggie was about to answer, when she heard a noise from the hall. She glanced around and found Davey standing there, tears in his eyes. "Davey, what's wrong?" she asked, hurrying toward him. "Are you not feeling well?"

The boy broke into a sob. "Mom, I feel so bad over what happened tonight. Jason promised not to tell, but I won't be able to sleep until I get it off my chest."

Jason knew he had been caught. You couldn't keep secrets from a mother no matter how hard you tried.

the night. "Were you going into Central
Grand Avenue told you this trip ... Then — I'd all begun.
I didn't want you to think you couldn't trust me
to take care of your children."

Anna crossed in front of her. Maggie's attention
was fixed on the street. She offered down a cursory
smile. "You didn't feel the need? I would have

Seven

By the time Davey had confessed his crimes to Maggie, Jason felt like crawling under a rock. A very *large* rock, far away, where he didn't have to look into Maggie's green eyes and explain how he had managed to lose one of her children. He shoved his hands deep in his pockets and regarded her.

"I'm sorry, Maggie. I guess I let you down. I should have told you the truth, but—" He shrugged. "I didn't want you to think you couldn't trust me to take care of your children."

Arms crossed in front of her, Maggie's attention was fixed on her son. She offered Jason a cursory glance. "You didn't let me down. I would have allowed Davey to go to a few houses with his friends as long as he promised to meet me afterward. Davey is the one at fault for not holding up his end of the bargain. Why did you do it, son?"

The boy hesitated a moment before answering. "'Cause I'm tired of everybody calling me a sissy," he said, his bottom lip trembling.

"Who's calling you a sissy?"

"My friends."

"They must not be very *good* friends."

"It's true, Mom," he said defensively. "I'm surrounded by girls all the time. You treat me like one of them. It's not fair!"

"Not fair?" Maggie pressed her face closer to her son's. "I'll tell you what's not fair, young man. Your three sisters are sharing one room, and I'm sharing a bed with Molly so you can have your own room. I'm doing everything I can to help you in soccer. Don't tell *me* I treat you like a girl! Don't tell *me* you don't get treated fairly in this house."

"You're doing this soccer stuff only to impress Jason."

"What?"

Jason shoved his hands more deeply into his pockets. He had never felt so uncomfortable. "Maybe I should leave, Maggie."

"You don't even *like* soccer," Davey accused his mother.

"But I *love* you," she said. "And it's because I love you so much that I'm determined to learn more about the game."

"You weren't that excited about it till you saw *my coach*," he said, cutting angry eyes to Jason.

"Now *you're* being unfair, Davey."

"It's true, Mom. And Jason took a *real* interest in me before he met you."

"I'm still interested in you, Davey," Jason interrupted. "This has nothing to do with your mother."

"Oh, yeah? Then how come you let me play goalie when I'm not even good at it?"

"Because I know you *can* be good if you put your mind to it."

"The kids say you're letting me play 'cause you've got the hots for my mom."

Maggie raised her hand, and without stopping

to think about it, slapped her son squarely in the face. A stunned silence followed. Suddenly Maggie was trembling. She had never slapped a child in the face before. She had always been able to remain calm and cool—until now.

"You hit me!" he accused her, raising his hand to his cheek. "See what I mean about you treating me like a baby. I wish I lived with Dad!"

The stricken look on Maggie's face was more than Jason could stand. He stepped forward. "That's enough, Davey," he said. "If you want to be treated like a man, then you're going to have to learn how to treat a lady. I think we've all said enough for one night, don't you?"

The boy was speechless for a moment. "You can't tell me what to do," he blurted out. "You're not my father."

"But I'm your coach," he said. "And since you're in training, I say it's high time you were in bed."

"You are *not* my coach anymore, 'cause I quit!"

"Davey!" Maggie could not believe what she was hearing.

"I quit," Davey repeated a bit more loudly.

"Then go ahead and quit," Jason told him. "But don't go blaming your mother because you can't cut the mustard, boy."

"Jason, please." Maggie felt *more* than enough had been said.

"It's true, Maggie. This has nothing to do with us. Davey is letting petty jealousies between his teammates get to him, shake his confidence. He's afraid he can't do it."

"I am not!" the boy shouted.

"You can't fail by trying, Davey. You can fail only when you give up. Quitters are failures. It's up to you."

Tears sprang to the boy's eyes. "You don't know what you're talking about!"

"I know what it's like to want to fit in with others, Davey. I didn't fit in very well when I was growing up, because none of the kids wanted to play at my house when we had to talk quietly and keep my room neat all the time." He paused. "And I know what it's like to want to spend more time with your dad," he said softly. "Mine was always too busy to play with me too. Until a few years ago," he added. "I suppose that's why I enjoy coaching so much."

"This isn't about you, Jason," Davey said. "It's about me." He left the room without another word.

Neither Maggie nor Jason said anything for a moment. They simply stood and listened to Davey's retreating footsteps and finally his bedroom door closing at the end of the hall. Maggie sighed and sank into the chair nearest her. "I'm sorry you had to go through that," she said. "I never realized how angry Davey was with me."

Jason shrugged. "I don't know, Maggie. The kid sounds peeved with both of us." He stepped closer and gazed down at her. "Letting Davey play goalie has nothing to do with you, though," he said. "It was a personal decision for me." He paused and glanced toward the empty hall. "I think I saw myself in him, the loneliness I knew growing up."

Maggie looked up at him and smiled, though her eyes were filled with tears. "I try to do my best with him, Jason. I do more for him than the girls, but it's never enough." She swallowed. A single tear fell to her cheek, and she wiped it away. "Davey has never had a lot of self-confidence. I thought if I got him interested in sports, that would change. Instead, it looks as though it's made things worse."

"It's not our fault the other boys are teasing him. That's the way kids are."

"How can you say it's not our fault? Davey's teammates think you're showing favoritism because of me."

"Well, it's not true. I was interested in Davey before I ever laid eyes on you."

"But I got in the way."

"What's that supposed to mean?"

"Davey shouldn't have to share you with me. After all, you were *his* friend first."

"Are you saying that I can't be friends with *both* of you?" When she didn't answer, he shook his head in disbelief. "That's the most ridiculous thing I've ever heard, Maggie."

"It's not so ridiculous to Davey."

"Then it's up to us to make him understand."

"I need time to think about this some more. I don't want to make any decisions tonight. I'm tired."

"Have dinner with me tomorrow, then. My place. Just the two of us. We can talk."

"I don't know."

"Don't walk away from me, Maggie," he said, taking her hand. "Don't give up on us so easily."

"I have to consider my son's feelings."

"What about mine? Don't they count?"

"I need time to think, Jason."

Jason knew he would waste his time arguing with her now. "Okay, I'll leave." He headed toward the door, his face resigned. Damned if it wasn't always something. Why couldn't he and Maggie simply enjoy what they had. "Call me and let me know about dinner."

• • •

Maggie forced a cheerfulness to her voice as she walked through Jason's door the following night, carrying a bottle of inexpensive red wine. "Something smells wonderful," she said.

Jason noticed right away how weary she looked. He had not slept very well the night before after the scene with Davey, and from the looks of it, neither had she. "I'm making my famous spaghetti," he announced, trying to match her lighthearted tone. "I brought the recipe over from the old country."

"The old country, huh?" She thought he looked wonderful as usual in his faded denims and comfortable pullover shirt. "I didn't know West Palm Beach was famous for its Italian cuisine." She handed him the bottle. "I brought something to go with the meal. I'm sure it's an excellent vintage. I bought it on sale at the convenience store down the street."

He chuckled, and their gazes met and locked. "I was afraid you wouldn't come."

She glanced away, feeling the tension mount between them. She felt guilty for being there. "I almost didn't."

With her face averted, he studied her profile: stubborn chin, turned-up nose, sooty lashes. "I didn't answer the phone today because I was afraid you'd cancel. I even turned off my answering machine."

A smile threatened the grim line of her mouth. "I know."

So she *had* tried to back out on him. "Here, let me take your sweater," he said, helping her out of it. It was still warm from her body. As he folded it once and draped it over the back of a chair, he caught the faint scent of her perfume.

"Why don't you join me in the kitchen," he suggested. "You can keep me company while I finish the salad."

Maggie followed him into the small kitchen, where he opened the bottle of wine she'd purchased. "To the old country," he said, raising his filled glass in a toast.

"The old country," she said, clinking her glass with his.

"Hey, this isn't half bad," Jason told her once he'd tasted the wine. "Let me find you something to sit on." He reached into a compact broom closet and pulled out a stepladder, then unfolded it. "You get the front-row seat tonight, how's that? And if you're nice, I'll teach you the secret to my homemade spaghetti sauce." He waited until she was settled. "Now, then. First I start with fresh tomatoes."

He was trying his best to ease the tension between them, she knew. "Fresh tomatoes? I'm impressed."

He regarded her, and for a moment he felt the old camaraderie return. No matter what, he would always like her. He'd sensed a bond from the beginning. Not that he had ever figured out why. Their lives were too different for it to be based on common ground. It didn't matter. The bond was there. "And so you should be." He glanced at her, and the smile faded. "So how's everything at home?"

"Davey's still sulking. He insists he's not going back to soccer."

"What did he say about your coming here tonight?"

Maggie didn't quite meet his gaze. "He doesn't know."

"What do you mean, he doesn't know?"

"He's staying with his father tonight. Without his sisters, for a change." She offered him a wry smile. "Could we get back to the cooking lesson, please?"

"Okay." He didn't need a brick wall to fall on him to know that she didn't want to talk about it. He could hear the strain in her voice, see it in her eyes. For once he wished she would let it all out, throw herself into his arms and admit to him that, yes, life sometimes got to be too much for her and yes, she *did* need him a little bit. But he knew her stubborn pride wouldn't allow it. So, once again he was forced to back off. "Now, once I find the right tomatoes, I blanch and peel them and cook 'em down—"

"Should I be taking notes?" she asked.

"I can give you a copy of my recipe later. Anyway, I use only fresh ingredients. Nothing from a can, mind you." He went on to explain each detail, even as he put the finishing touches on a big salad. Still, he didn't want to discuss his spaghetti recipe any more than he wanted to know how she got grape-juice stains out of her carpet. He wanted to talk about *them*, find out where they stood after this latest incident with Davey. There was always something standing in their way, he reminded himself. Some force trying to keep them apart.

Maggie watched Jason crumble several slices of crisp bacon over the salad greens. His hands never failed to mesmerize. They were big and masculine but surprisingly graceful. She knew they could be tender as well. Those same hands had wiped away Molly's milk mustaches, struggled with the twins' knotted shoelaces, and offered an encouraging pat on the back to her son. Something fluttered in Maggie's stomach as she wondered what it would be like to have those hands touching *her*, those fingers caressing her cheek, her breasts. The mere thought made her shiver. She pushed the image aside, knowing she would never get through the evening if she didn't. "You must enjoy cooking to go through all this trouble," she said after a minute. "My spaghetti sauce comes from a jar."

"It doesn't always seem worth it for one person." He shrugged. "I always have tons of leftovers. How about you? Do you like to cook?"

"I used to. In fact, I once took a gourmet cooking class. But I really don't have time to do all that fancy stuff nowadays." She smiled. "We eat a lot of meat loaf and casserole dishes at our house."

"So what else do you like to do when you're not working and caring for children?"

"I sleep."

"Besides that."

She chuckled. "Face it. I have no life outside of my job and the children."

"Now you do," he said, then wished he hadn't when her smile faded abruptly. Once again the silence stretched between them—tense, broken only by the intermittent bubbling of simmering tomato sauce.

"I don't know, Jason," she said on a weary sigh.

He could sense she was backing off. Again. She reminded him of a timid sparrow he'd tried to catch in the back of the boarding school. He and several other boys had fashioned a trap of sorts, propped one corner on a stick, then ran a long cord through the window of their dorm. The little sparrow had eaten every last seed surrounding the trap, but never came within reach. Maggie, like the sparrow, was determined not to get too close. "You're not still having doubts about us, are you?" he said, trying not to let his distress show. Would she stop seeing him because her son was jealous? he wondered. He turned to her, wiping his hands on a towel, not because they were dirty but because he felt he needed to do something with them to keep from reaching out to her. "You can't let a child force a decision like that."

He didn't have to clarify the statement for her. "This isn't *any* child, Jason. This is my son."

"We can work it out, Maggie darlin'. I can talk to Davey, spend more time with him."

"I never wanted to involve my children in this or any relationship."

"In case it doesn't work out, right?" He gave her a knowing look. When she didn't answer he tossed the dishtowel aside and regarded her, hands on hips. He could sense her withdrawal. Which meant he had nothing to lose by confronting her. "Why don't you level with me, Maggie. It's not your children you're worried about. You're concerned about your own skin." She opened her mouth to protest, but he cut her off. "And don't try to deny it, it's all over your face. You're running scared. You're letting one man influence the rest of your life. You say you no longer feel anything for Bob Farnsworth, but look at the power he still has over you."

"That's not true!"

"I would never have figured you for a coward."

Maggie jumped up from the ladder. "You don't know what you're talking about."

"Then tell me, for heaven's sake!" he all but shouted.

"I don't want to have to depend on another

person for my happiness. Is that so hard to understand?" She didn't give him time to answer. "Because, when it's over, I always end up alone." Her
eyes teared. "At first it's terrifying. Then, after a
while you become hardened. Determined to make
it alone. I *know* I can make it on my own now,
Jason. I'm stronger. I don't ever want to lose that."

"Who took those things from you, Maggie? Was
it Bob?"

She nodded, and the tears fell. "He was one of
them. He made me believe I could trust him."

"So, we both agree he's a bastard. Whose the
other guy?"

"My father."

He blinked in surprise. "Your father?"

She sank back onto the ladder. "He died when I
was twelve years old. A massive heart attack. Here
one minute, gone the next. I never even got to say
good-bye."

Jason didn't know what to say. He shoved his
hands into his pockets. Once again he wanted to
reach out to her. Once again he resisted. "I'm
sorry."

She shrugged and wiped her tears. "That wasn't
the worst part, Jason. My mother was devastated.
She didn't know the first thing about taking care
of a family. She had a nervous breakdown. My
younger sister and I had to make even the small-
est decisions for her. We learned at an early age
that it was up to us to take care of things." She
paused and shook her head sadly. "I kept thinking
when I got married it would be different. Easier.
I would have the big happy family I'd always
wanted. But it didn't turn out that way. Bob
walked out when Molly was less than a year old."
She paused and took a deep, shuddering breath.

"So I decided then and there that I would *never* depend on anyone again." She eyed him steadily. "Especially a younger man who might get restless after a while and leave."

Jason pondered all she'd said. Once again they were silent. "You were wrong about one thing, Maggie," he said at last.

"What's that?"

"You *are* a coward after all," he said gently.

She felt her cheeks burn with indignation. "You have no right to say that about me!"

"You claim to be so tough, but you don't fool me. You're afraid to care for a man because you're terrified he'll leave and hurt you, not your kids." He stepped closer, reached for her, but she shrugged him off.

"You know what your problem is?" she said. "You're so used to getting what you want from women that you're totally baffled when one doesn't fall for that good ol' boy charm of yours."

"Oh, you've fallen for it, all right. You just refuse to believe it."

"Give me a break, Jason."

"I have. But I'm tired of being so damned patient with you. I've tried everything possible to get close. I've given one hundred percent, Maggie. But I can't build a future with someone who still has so many leftover grudges from the past."

"You're wrong," she said. "I may allow events from my past to influence my decisions to an extent, but I also depend on plain old common sense. And common sense tells me that no matter how nice you are and how attractive I find you, I have absolutely no business getting involved with you."

"Ah-ha! So you do admit that you find me attractive."

With that she headed out of the room. Unfortunately, Jason was in the way, and she found herself doing a little jig in order to get past him. "Would you please move," she said, growing more frustrated with every breath she took.

"Where are you going?"

"Home."

"You can't go home. I've spent all afternoon cooking dinner for us."

She finally pushed past him. "You should have thought of that before you started playing analyst with me."

She was already at the door, and there wasn't a blasted thing he could do to stop her. Damn stubborn woman! She was looking for a reason to leave. Any excuse would do. "Okay, so go!" he said so loud it brought Maggie to a skidding halt. In a fit of frustration, he picked up the dishtowel, wadded it up, and hurled it across the room.

Maggie blinked as the towel made contact with the wall in a dull thump and slid to the floor. She swung her gaze in Jason's direction and saw that his chest was literally heaving with pent-up emotion.

"Well, what are you waiting for? There's the door. Go ahead and check out, lady. That's all you've wanted to do from the beginning."

Suddenly she felt awful for him. For herself. She was crazy about the man. So why was she always pushing him away? Maybe he was right. Maybe she *was* a coward. "I don't have to go this very minute," she said. "Perhaps we could talk."

He shook his head, then waved her off as though ready to be done with her. "I'm tired of talking. I'm tired of pretending." He went back into the kitchen.

Maggie followed, her coppery brows puckered into a worried frown. She didn't like the sound of his voice. He was giving up on her. She suddenly felt more frightened than she had in a long time. At the same time, she didn't blame him. If only she could stop rehashing the past and fretting about the future and live for the present. "What do you mean, you're tired of pretending?"

Jason picked up a spoon and began stirring the spaghetti sauce so fast, it sloshed over the sides of the pot, sizzling and spitting as it hit the burner. He turned it off. "I'm tired of pretending I'm comfortable with this relationship when I'm not. I keep telling myself to be patient, that sooner or later you'll warm up to me, learn to trust me. But you're as skittish as you were the night I met you."

"What do you expect from me, Jason?"

He put down the spoon and faced her. "I expect honesty, Maggie."

"Honesty?"

"I expect you to acknowledge what you feel for me." He paused. "Of course, I may be reading you all wrong. Maybe you don't feel anything. If that's the case, I'm wasting my time."

Maggie didn't answer right away. "I don't know what to say, Jason. Maybe you were right," she said, going with her previous thought. "Maybe I am a coward after all."

"What are you so afraid of?" he demanded.

She hesitated. "I'm afraid of falling in love with you, of needing you. I thought I had done rather well without all that in my life, but I suppose I was only fooling myself." Her eyes filled with fresh tears. "I just don't get it. I'm surrounded by five children, and I've never felt more alone in my life."

Jason felt his heart turn over in his chest at the sight of her tears. "Oh, Maggie." He went to her, taking her into his arms. "You don't have to be alone, darlin'." She buried her face against his chest, and he cupped the back of her head with his palm. She felt small and vulnerable in his arms, and he was suddenly filled with the need to protect her, watch over her, keep her safe. She lifted her tear-streaked face, and the next thing he knew he was kissing her damp eyelids and wondering if he had ever felt skin so soft. The translucent lids were fringed with long lashes that fell like half-moons over her cheekbones. He kissed her temple and felt her welcoming pulse against his lips. He kissed her nose, the dimple in her chin, then pressed his mouth to the hollow of her throat. She didn't offer any resistance. And finally, he captured her mouth.

Maggie was not sure how long the kiss lasted. All she was aware of at the moment was how wonderful Jason tasted, how good he smelled, how solid his chest felt against hers. Solid and comforting. She pressed closer, and when he parted her lips with his tongue, she was only too happy to accommodate him. He explored her mouth thoroughly, leaving no area untouched. He skimmed her teeth, then dipped inside and mated with her own shy tongue. Each gentle foray tugged at her insides. She felt his hands caress the small of her back, and she shivered. He continued to kiss her until she was weak-kneed and trembling, until her lower belly felt warm, until she realized, all at once, she was pressing against him. She was embarrassed at her own eager response.

Jason broke the kiss and gazed down at her. "Maggie darlin', this is getting out of control," he said, his voice raspy in her ear. "If we don't stop now—" He paused, and his gaze remained fixed on her trembling lips. The desire to kiss them was as strong as his desire to take in oxygen.

Maggie took a deep, shaky breath. "I don't want to stop," she said at last.

She saw the answer in his eyes with lightning-quick speed. He captured her mouth once more with a hunger that surprised and delighted her. Finally, he raised his head, swept her high in his arms, and carried her into the bedroom.

Eight

The room was dim, save for the light that spilled in from the living room and cast a soft glow on Jason's face. Everything else was swathed in shadows. In the semidarkness Maggie saw that Jason's eyes were the color of sapphires. Under any other circumstances she would have been anxious. But the look on his face was so sincere, so sweet, she knew everything would be okay.

"Are you nervous?" he asked as though reading her mind.

"A little."

"You shouldn't be," he whispered, brushing his lips against hers. "This is the best part."

Maggie felt herself being lowered onto the bed, felt the mattress dip beneath his weight as he joined her. Once again Jason took her into his arms. This time when he kissed her she responded eagerly, parting her lips and taking his tongue deep inside. His mouth was warm and tasted of the wine he'd just sipped—sweet and delicious and just as intoxicating. Maggie suspected she could quickly become drunk on his kisses.

Finally, Jason broke the kiss, and they both drank in a deep breath. His lips reappeared at her temples, her fluttering lids, pressing damp kisses against the translucent skin. Maggie moaned softly and gave in to the sheer pleasure of being in his arms.

Soon, kisses weren't enough. Maggie was vaguely aware of the tension building low in her belly. She didn't realize how hungry she was for Jason until he reached for the buttons of her blouse. She was only too happy to oblige, her sense of modesty taking a backseat to desire. Even without her blouse her skin felt hot and flushed. Nevertheless, she shivered when Jason pressed his lips below her collarbone.

Jason began undressing her with painstaking slowness. He unfastened her bra, then slid the straps down her arms—slowly, leisurely, as though he had all night to accomplish this one act. His lips followed, kissing the tender flesh of the insides of her arms, the insides of her elbows, and finally her inner wrist. Her arms tingled in response.

"Look at you, Maggie," Jason whispered, his tone reverent as he gazed at her breasts. They were the breasts of a mature woman: full and round with thick coral-tipped nipples. He wondered if she had nursed her babies at those breasts, and the thought that she had made him feel all the more loving toward her. "You're beautiful," he said at last, then lowered his head as if bowing before her.

Maggie sucked her breath in sharply as Jason took one rose-crested breast between his lips and flirted with it, flicking it lightly with his tongue, nipping it with his teeth. She could feel the sensations deep inside. She grasped his head between her hands and held him fast, enjoying the feel of his roughened jaw against her flesh. Her skin prickled, her limbs felt weighted. But low in her belly a knot of anticipation was growing into something urgent and hot. Jason moved against her, and she felt his hardness at her thighs. Her passion flared.

Clothes quickly became a hindrance that Maggie was as eager to be free of as Jason. They didn't slow down until they both lay naked beside each other.

"Oh, Maggie," he said. "You take my breath away."

She gazed up at him with emotion-packed eyes, thinking she had never seen anything as magnificent as Jason Profitt, lean and perfectly sculptured, feathered with the same golden hair that covered his head. When he looked at her, it was easy to forget she was the mother of five and older than he. She felt young and beautiful. She felt desired. Then he stroked her thighs and all logical thought ceased. Again his mouth possessed hers hungrily, his tongue greedy for what lay past her lips. He skimmed her thighs once more before wedging his hand between them and seeking out her femininity. He smiled when his fingers found her wet and warm. He dipped inside and explored, and Maggie was lost.

Moaning softly against the wondrous sensations his touch created, Maggie thrashed her head from side to side and called out to him. She could feel the pressure building. It was as wonderful as it was unbearable. Her body was sensitized, attuned to his every movement, to each ragged breath he took. She squirmed and strained against him, waiting to be filled, eager to put an end to the restless need. Finally, Jason parted her knees and entered her, and Maggie felt as though she had been swallowed up in something more powerful than life itself. She arched and met each thrust, encouraged by the throaty whispers at her ear.

Desire coursed through her body. Maggie cried out softly as it sent her over the edge into a sweet abyss. Jason followed, shuddering in her arms, chanting her name over and over like the words of a favorite song.

Afterward, there was no need for words. Maggie curled against his wide chest and closed her eyes, knowing she would never be quite the same.

When Maggie opened her eyes sometime later, she had no idea where she was. She shifted in the bed and found herself lying next to Jason. As though sensing she was now awake, he opened his eyes and smiled the smile of a satisfied man. "Hi."

Maggie blinked, coming wide awake at the sight of him and the realization of where she was. Jason Profitt's bed! She glanced around the room quickly, panic filling the back of her throat. How different things looked when one's eyes weren't blurred with passion. She swallowed. Her mouth was bone dry. "What time is it?"

Jason wrenched his neck around to where an alarm clock sat on his nightstand. "It's after midnight." He chuckled. "Looks like we were out for a few hours."

Maggie bolted straight up in the bed. "Midnight!" She glanced at the clock and saw that he was right. "Oh, no!" She threw off the covers, swung her legs over the side of the bed, and fumbled for her clothes, thankful for the dark in her state of nakedness. "Why didn't you wake me!"

Jason raised up slowly. "I fell asleep too," he said. "I guess we were both tired." He rubbed his eyes. "Were you supposed to be home by a certain time?"

Maggie was frantic. "I promised my sitter I'd be home by eleven. Have you seen my blouse?"

Jason scrambled off the bed and turned on the lamp. Maggie shrank away in modesty. He grinned. "It's too late for that, Maggie darlin'," he said, sweeping her blouse off the floor and handing it to her. "I've already seen everything you've got." Still, he let his eyes take in each gentle curve as though viewing it for the first time. With her cheeks flaming the color of overripe tomatoes, Maggie dressed in record-breaking time. "I can't believe we slept three hours," she muttered under her breath as she hurried out the bedroom door.

Jason followed. "What about dinner?"

"I don't have time to eat." Maggie shoved her feet into her sneakers, then searched for her purse. She found it on the dining room table. She turned for the door and literally slammed into Jason, who was in the process of fastening his jeans.

"Look, why don't you call your sitter and tell her you're going to be a little late?" he suggested. "I don't want you driving home like a crazy woman."

"I can't do that," she said as though it were the most ridiculous thing she'd ever heard. "I promised I'd be there." She strode toward the front door with the zeal of a fireman on the heels of a three alarm fire.

"I'm sure she'll understand once you explain," he said.

Maggie faced him. "Explain what, Jason? That I fell asleep in your bed? No, I don't think so."

"Look, Maggie, I can already see those little wheels turning in your head. I don't want you to feel guilty about this. What happened between us—"

But she was already out the door. She all but raced to the car and squealed out of the parking lot a moment later as though the devil himself were after her.

Maggie sped home, one eye on the road, the other fixed on the rearview mirror, hoping and praying there were no patrol cars around. The last thing she needed was a speeding ticket. She pulled into her driveway ten minutes later, unlocked her front door, and hurried in. Her sitter was asleep on the couch. She woke the girl, then walked her the half-block home, apologizing along the way before rushing back to her house. It was already one o'clock in the morning. She had just climbed into bed when the telephone rang. She grabbed it on the first ring so it wouldn't wake Molly, who was sleeping beside her. Jason spoke from the other end.

"Maggie, it's me. Is everything okay?"

"Yes," she whispered. "The girl probably won't sit for me again, but I got her home safely."

"I'm sorry. Not for what happened between us, but for making you late." When she didn't answer, he went on. "I hope you don't have any regrets."

"Look, Jason, I don't know how I feel right now. I mean, it was wonderful and all—" She paused. Wonderful didn't even come close. It was out of this world. Her toes were still numb. She didn't say as much to Jason. "But there's still the problem of my son, and everything else. That's not likely to change. I need time."

"I'm not going to let go, Maggie. Our fate was

sealed in my bed tonight, sweetheart. We belong together. Despite your fears, despite your son."

"Yes, Jason, but—"

"No buts. I'm coming after you, Maggie, with both barrels, and there's not a damn thing you can do about it. I'm going to sweep you off your feet, and I'm going to see you in my bed again real soon. Think about it." He hung up.

Maggie stared at the phone in disbelief for a full minute before hanging up. Only then did she notice her trembling fingers.

Whispers.

Maggie ignored them and snuggled more deeply beneath the covers. Someone giggled. She opened her eyes and found, much to her horror, Jason and her girls standing at the foot of her bed. She was obviously dreaming.

"Good morning," he said.

No, it wasn't a dream at all. Nothing but the real thing looked and smelled that good. Maggie bolted upright in the bed, dragging her bedcovers with her. "What are you doing here!" she demanded. More giggles.

"I'm taking you and your lovely girls to breakfast. Everybody's dressed but you." He clucked his tongue and wagged his finger in her face as though she were indeed the naughtiest thing he'd come across in a long time.

Maggie stared back in silence at the group. Her daughters were dressed neatly, every hair in place. Even Molly, whose hair was *seldom* in place. "How long have you been here?" she asked.

"Not that long. When I told everybody we were going out to eat, they scrambled to get ready. Now, how soon can *you* be ready? We're starved."

"Well, I can't very well get dressed with all of you standing there," she said, suddenly self-conscious about how she must look without an ounce of makeup and her hair falling all over her head as though she'd been caught in a serious windstorm. Jason was freshly shaven, wearing nicely pressed slacks and a blue shirt that looked as though it had been cast into the same dye as his eyes. Wasn't it just like a man to look that good in the morning! She resisted the urge to pull the covers over her head.

Jason's gaze fell to her lips, and it was obvious he was thinking about the previous night. Maggie felt a hot blush crawl up her neck, but she refused to give in to her state of embarrassment and glared back at him instead. "Okay, we can take a hint, can't we, girls?" he said to her daughters. More giggles. "Come on, troop, let's clear the room so your mother can get ready." He winked at Maggie. "Call me if you need any help." The blush spread to her scalp.

Maggie didn't waste any time once she was alone. She jumped in the shower, washed in record time, then pulled on a pair of slacks and lightweight sweater. All the while she thought of the man in the next room, who had managed to win the hearts of four little girls. The sweet-talker, she thought with a snort. That's what he was.

Our fate was sealed in my bed tonight, sweetheart, he'd told her over the phone the night before. "I'm coming after you with both barrels." She had tossed and turned in her bed, wondering what that meant exactly. And then she had worried about her son some more.

Hurrying as fast as she could, she put on a minimum amount of makeup, dried her hair under the blow dryer, and dashed down the hall, where she found Jason and the girls waiting impatiently in the living room.

"I can't leave until I find out what Davey is going to do," she said breathlessly. She made her way into the kitchen and picked up the phone. When she returned to the living room she was frowning. "Davey wants to spend another night with his father. Bob said he'll take him to school in the morning."

Jason didn't miss the fretful look in her eyes. "It'll do them both good, Maggie. Now, stop worrying and let's go."

There was something positively unnerving about looking into a man's face once you'd spent time in his bed, Maggie discovered. She suddenly felt shy and unsure of herself. "Are you sure you want to go through with this?" she asked him. "You've never taken four children out to breakfast."

He grinned back. "I'm no wimp. Come on." He herded the group toward the door. "Oh, by the way, we'll have to take your car. Mine's not big enough."

Maggie fumbled in her purse for her keys, then dropped them twice. They bumped heads reaching for them at the same time. She blushed. "Maybe you should drive."

"Good idea." It was obvious he was amused with her nervousness and knew exactly what it was about.

Once everybody was loaded into the car, Jason drove to a nearby restaurant. "We need a big table," he told the hostess as they all filed inside. The woman led them to a circular booth at the back and passed out menus while Maggie did her best to keep the girls quiet. When the waitress arrived and saw the tableful of kids, the look on her face told them she'd rather be someplace else.

But Maggie was used to that look. No doubt the woman was already dreading the mess they'd make. What neither woman was prepared for was Jason's charm. He turned it on full blast, and by the time the waitress took their order, she was all smiles.

"Thanks, Shirley," Jason told the woman, reading the name tag she wore. He handed her their menus, and she hurried away, still smiling.

"You really pour it on thick when you have to, don't you?" Maggie said under her breath. He grinned in response.

"How would you like to go to the zoo today?" Jason asked once they had all been served breakfast. The girls nodded enthusiastically. Everyone except for Maggie.

"It's an hour's drive from here," she pointed out.

"Is that a problem?"

"You obviously haven't taken many long drives with a carload of children."

Jason regarded the girls with a baffled look. "Your mother seems to think you won't behave yourself in the car," he said.

"We'll be good," the twins said in unison.

"And not fuss," Jessie promised.

"Or make you stop more than once for the bathroom," Molly offered.

"They'll be good," Jason told Maggie confidently.

When they returned home at the end of the day, dragging four exhausted children from the car, Jason offered to run out for sandwich meat while Maggie supervised baths and got things ready for school and work the following morning. By the time she had Molly in her pajamas, Jason had prepared a plateful of sandwiches and was tear-ing into a large potato-chip bag. Even though it wasn't quite eight o'clock, the whole group looked tired. It had been a full day. Once they'd finished at the zoo, Jason had taken them out for hamburgers, then to the city park, where they had rented paddle boats and raced back and forth across the small lake.

Now, gazing at the sleepy bunch, Maggie couldn't remember when they had all had more fun. She only wished her son had been there to enjoy it as well. As soon as they finished eating, she herded Molly and the twins into the bathroom to brush their teeth while Jason straightened the kitchen. Although Jessie was allowed to stay up an hour later than her siblings, she was more than happy to go to bed early. Maggie was thankful for the quiet time.

"Looks like it's just you and me left," Jason said when they were alone. "What would you say to a cup of coffee before I go? Jessie showed me where to find the filters while you were bathing Molly, so I made some. It should be ready."

Maggie nodded. "As long as we can drink it on the sofa with our feet up," she said, kicking off her sneakers. "We must've walked ten miles today."

"At least *you* didn't have to carry Molly," he pointed out.

"That's true." She grinned ruefully. "I suppose the least I can do is pour the coffee." She disappeared into the kitchen, then returned a few minutes later with two steaming mugs.

"Just set my cup down," Jason told her with a yawn. "I don't think I have the strength to lift it at the moment."

Maggie chuckled. "I told you they were a handful." She set her own cup beside his and joined him on the couch, propping her feet on the coffee table and convincing Jason to do the same. They simply sat there for a moment in a comfortable silence.

"Where do you reckon they get all that energy?" he asked after a moment.

Maggie shook her head. The sofa felt wonderful. "Lord only knows."

Jason yawned and stretched, then put one arm around her so that she could lean against him. "If only we could find a way to bottle it—"

"And use it for ourselves." Maggie smiled as she said it, turning her head slightly in order to see him. He was watching her, a thoughtful expression on his face. She wondered if he was thinking about the previous night, the lovemaking they'd shared. She had thought of little else all day. And every time she thought about it or looked into those gorgeous blue eyes of his, her stomach fluttered wildly, and she ached to hold him and be held by him again. It was scary wanting a man that badly.

"I had a great time today, darlin'." He leaned close and pressed his lips against her forehead.

She was about to answer when she heard a sound from her bedroom. "It's Molly," she said, recognizing the sound immediately. She pushed herself up from the couch. "Her stomach was bothering her when I put her to bed. Probably too much cotton candy."

"Not to mention popcorn and peanuts," he mumbled.

"I'd better go check on her. Don't forget about your coffee."

Maggie found Molly sitting up in her bed when she entered the room. "Is your tummy still bothering you, honey?" she asked.

The little girl shook her head. "I'm thirsty."

Maggie brought her a glass of water from the bathroom, then sat with her daughter for a few minutes until she drifted off to sleep. Finally, Maggie pulled the covers beneath Molly's chin and slipped from the room.

"She wanted a drink of water," she told Jason when she returned to the living room. "I think it was the excitement of the day." She came to an abrupt halt when she spied him on the sofa sound asleep. His coffee was untouched. Smiling to herself, she picked up her own cup, took the chair next to the sofa, and sipped while she listened to Jason's gentle snoring. It had been a long time since a man had slept in her house, she thought, noting the peaceful rise and fall of his chest. She listened to the sound, and it soothed her like no music could.

Of course, the best thing to do was wake him. Tomorrow was Monday, a workday for them both. Jason would need to be up early. But the longer she sat and watched the sleeping man, the less inclined she was to wake him and send him out into the night. Even as she thought it, she knew she was fooling herself. It wasn't as if she lived in the Arctic and was about to send him on his way in blizzard conditions in a broken-down sled driven by lame huskies. "Face it, Maggie," she whispered to herself. "You don't *want* him to go."

Perhaps she'd set the alarm clock thirty minutes early in order to give him time to drive home when he awoke, she told herself. Maggie drained her cup and set it back on the table next to Jason's. It looked good sitting there. For four years now hers had been the only cup on the kitchen table, hers the only slippers beside her bed. Finally, she went to the hall closet and pulled out a blanket and pillow. Very gently she tucked the pillow beneath his blond head and covered him. She studied his face. He really was a handsome devil, she thought as she resisted the urge to kiss him. Much too handsome to burden himself with a woman with five children.

Maggie sighed softly to herself as she made her way down the hall toward her bedroom. It wasn't until she was in bed that she allowed herself to deal with the guilty feelings that had suddenly taken hold of her. She *did* feel guilty about her relationship with Jason, she realized. She felt guilty that she was older with one marriage behind her and five children to raise, while Jason had everything ahead of him.

Jason deserved better, she told herself. He deserved a woman who didn't come with a ready-made family and responsibilities. He deserved a child of his own. It was wrong to rob him of those things.

But what could she do, Maggie asked herself now. She was falling in love with the man. She was jolted to the soles of her feet by the sudden realization that she was indeed in love with Jason Profitt. She loved him! She loved the way he teased her about taking life too seriously. She loved the way he took pleasure in the simple things in her life, the way he encouraged her to include her children in what they did together when most men would have resented them. And she loved the way he made her feel when he held her, made love to her.

But how could she expect such a relationship to last? she asked herself. Right now their feelings for each other were new and exciting. What would it be like after that newness wore off? Would Jason always be willing to accept her children so easily? There were times when she wanted nothing more than a little peace and quiet, when she wanted to be as far away as possible from her children, and she loved them with all her heart. How could she expect Jason to deal with them day after day after day?

Maggie lay awake for a long time, pondering these things, wondering what the future held for her and the man in the next room. They should never have made love, she told herself. That had been the turning point for her, although she had subconsciously tried to deny it ever since. Jason claimed it had sealed their fate, that he was not going to be pushed away again. Even now, all she could think of was Jason holding her, Jason kissing her, Jason making love to her. Had her children not been in the house, she would have brought him to her bed. It frightened her, knowing how much she wanted him. Needed him.

Jason was already up when Maggie turned off the alarm clock and hurried into the living room the following morning. The couch was empty, his blanket folded neatly at one end. She found him in the kitchen, pouring coffee.

"Good morning," he said, fixing a cup for her as well. "I'm sorry I flaked out on you last night. You should have woke me."

Maggie took the cup he offered, noting the disheveled blond hair spilling over his forehead, his unshaven jaw. He was a sexy sight indeed. She smiled. "You looked so comfortable, I didn't have the heart. How'd you sleep?"

"Fine, considering I was alone," he said, and followed the comment with a leisurely kiss that told her he much preferred her company under the covers. He gazed at her from over the rim of his cup, thinking how pretty she looked, fresh from sleep. He wondered what it would be like to wake up next to her with the sun spilling on her face. "So what's the game plan?" he asked. "Want me to make breakfast? How about scrambled eggs and toast?" He was already moving toward the refrigerator. "By the way, how many eggs does it take to feed this crew?"

Maggie chuckled. "A lot. But I can do that. You have to drive home and get ready yourself."

He opened the refrigerator and peered inside, bringing out eggs and butter and a small block of cheese. "I've got plenty of time," he said. "Why don't you wake the girls. By the time they're dressed, I'll have breakfast made."

Maggie knew it was useless to argue. He was already fumbling beside the stove for a skillet. Smiling, she carried her coffee cup down the hall and knocked on the girls' bedroom door. Yes, there was something nice about having a man in the house, especially one as incredible as the hunk in the next room.

By the time the girls were dressed, Jason had a large platter of cheesy scrambled eggs on the table as well as a mountain of toast. Maggie was still running around in her robe.

"Go ahead and take your shower," Jason told her.

"I still have to make lunches."

"Jessie and I can do that." He prodded Maggie in the direction of the bedroom.

When Maggie returned freshly showered, she found the lunches finished, breakfast dishes stacked in the kitchen sink, and Jason on his way out the door, looking more like Prince Charming every time she saw him. "Thanks for everything," she said. "You really are a lifesaver."

He winked and tweaked her nose. "Have a good day, Maggie darlin'. I'll call you later."

And then he was gone. Maggie stood at the door in her robe and watched him pull out of the driveway, a faint smile on her lips. What a guy! When she turned around she found Jessie standing there, watching her curiously. "What is it, honey?" she said, blushing when she realized her oldest had caught her staring after a man with a lovesick expression on her face.

"Are you in love with Jason?" the girl asked.

Maggie was thankful the other children were busy, because she was not at all prepared for the question. "In love?" she asked her daughter. "That's a rather strong word."

"You are, aren't you?"

Maggie saw that Jessie wasn't about to budge until she had an answer. "Well, maybe I am just a little bit," she confessed at last. "Would that bother you?"

The girl looked thoughtful. "I guess I've been hoping all along that you and Daddy would get back together."

Maggie couldn't have been more surprised. "I'm sorry if I've said or done anything to make you think that, Jessie. Your father and I don't love each other anymore. We still love our children, of course, but—" She paused, palms splayed, not knowing what else to say.

"How did you fall *out* of love?"

Maggie saw that the girl truly wanted to know. "I don't know, honey," she said at last. "I suppose we grew apart. That sometimes happens between couples."

"Is there any way to keep it from happening?"

Maggie knew she needed to leave for work. Of all times for Jessie to want to talk. But this was important. "I'm sure there are things couples can do to keep their love alive, Jessie. If they want to badly enough. If the relationship is worth it."

"How do you know if it's worth it?"

"Well—" Maggie tried to think. "You know it's worth it if you can't stand being away from that person for very long."

"Is that how you feel about Jason?"

Maggie smiled. "I suppose I do," she said. She knew it was the truth. Already she was counting the hours until Jason called her or came by.

Jessie seemed to ponder it. "I'm happy for you, Mom," she said at last. "You need somebody. Us kids aren't going to be around forever, you know."

Maggie chuckled and hugged her daughter to herself. "Thanks for the warning, Jessie."

Nine

The telephone was ringing when Maggie walked into her office that morning. Bob was on the other end.

"We need to talk. Can you meet me for lunch this afternoon?"

Maggie knew a moment of panic. "Is something wrong with Davey?"

"No, I dropped him off at school this morning. He's fine. But he told me some things while he was here, and I think we should discuss them."

Maggie could think of about six dozen ways she'd rather spend her lunch hour than meeting her ex-husband. It was amazing that they had spent so many years together when now they couldn't be in a room five minutes without disagreeing. Which was why she avoided him at all cost. But something was obviously wrong for him to want to take up his precious time to see her.

"Okay," she said a bit reluctantly, and gave him the name of a coffeeshop near her office. "I'll see you at noon."

Maggie found herself looking up at the clock

every fifteen minutes until the time arrived for her to meet Bob. What could he possibly want?

At precisely five minutes before twelve she hurried out of her office and down the street to the coffeeshop, arriving a bit out of breath. Bob waved to her from a table in the back of the restaurant. She joined him, gave a waitress her order, then turned her full attention to her ex-husband.

"What did you want to see me about?"

"You're looking good, Maggie. It must be that new boyfriend of yours."

Maggie stiffened in her seat. So Davey had told Bob about Jason. "I didn't come here to discuss my personal life, Bob. If you have something to tell me about my son—"

"Oh, stop getting so defensive," he said, reaching across the table for her hand. He covered it with his own. "I think it's great you're finally seeing someone. I'm not sure Davey shares my enthusiasm, unfortunately."

Maggie pulled her hand free. "What did he say?"

"He asked if he could come live with me."

Maggie felt as though someone had reached inside her chest and twisted her heart. "Oh." She didn't know what to say. Finally gathering her wits, though, she met his gaze. "What did you tell him?"

"I told him it was up to you." He shrugged and looked away. "Actually, I didn't know *what* to say to the kid, Maggie. You know how difficult it would be for me to take him. Impossible, really, what with my having to travel and all."

"I wasn't aware you were traveling that much."

Another shrug. "I have to be away several times a month."

"I see." It was a lame excuse on his part, which meant he really didn't want his son with him in the first place. Maggie was relieved. She could not imagine letting the boy go. She offered the man a wry smile. "So you want me to tell Davey he can't live with you. Why do I always get stuck playing the villain? Why can't you simply explain it to him yourself?"

"It would sound better coming from you."

She sighed. "I doubt it. Davey isn't very happy with me at the moment."

"Yes, well, he feels his coach was more interested in him before you came along and stole his limelight."

"I didn't steal anything, and his coach is *still* very interested in him."

"Davey has trouble making friends, Maggie. We've always known that. I think he really likes this guy Jason. That's all he talked about when he first started playing soccer. It's a good confidence-boost for him."

"I don't know what to do," Maggie said, thinking out loud.

Bob shrugged. "I certainly don't want to tell you your business, Maggie, but unless this guy really means something to you . . ." He let the sentence drop.

She looked at him. "What?"

He shook his head. "Never mind."

"You were going to say I should stop seeing him."

"I can't make that decision for you."

"You're so good at this, Bob," she said stiffly. "Trying to make me feel guilty, that is."

"That is *not* what I'm trying to do. I'm merely trying to help you."

She laughed out loud. "Help me! By insinuating that I'm ruining my son's life by dating his soccer coach? By hinting that I should put my child's feelings before my own? What do you think I've been doing all these years?" When he didn't respond, she went on. "I *never* make a decision where I don't consider my children first and foremost. I can't believe you're sitting here passing judgment on me, Bob Farnsworth. And I can't believe I'm listening. You of all people have no right—"

"Here we go," he said with a weary sigh. "I knew I shouldn't have said anything."

"But you couldn't resist, could you? What's wrong, Bob, don't you enjoy seeing me happy? Am I not making *enough* sacrifices for our children?" She realized she was talking too loud, but she couldn't help it. Their conversation was drawing stares from the people next to them.

"I'm sorry if you feel encumbered by our children, Maggie, but they didn't ask to be put on this earth. You wanted a big family from the beginning. You even made me believe I wanted the same until I realized I was going to grow old before my time trying to make ends meet. Now that you're having to worry about the bills, it's gotten to be too much for you, hasn't it?"

"You really are a bastard, you know that?"

"Lower your voice, please."

Maggie stood so fast, she almost sent her chair toppling. "Get this straight, Bob. I make my own decisions. Don't ever try to tell me who I can or can't see, and don't tell me how to raise my children."

"*Your* children?"

"That's right. You've never once been there for them, not even when you were living under the same roof. I kept thinking you'd change, but you didn't. When's the last time you sacrificed for them? When's the last time you actually took money from your own pocket—"

"It all comes down to money with you, doesn't it?"

She leaned closer to him. "Damn right it does. When it comes to putting food in their stomachs and clothes on their backs, I care very much about the money. I can't count on you for anything. Has it ever occurred to you that *you* might be responsible for some of Davey's problems?"

"I have a life of my own now, Maggie. So sue me."

"I might just do that." She had the satisfaction of seeing the color drain from his face. "I'll see you in court." She turned and stalked out of the coffeeshop just as their waitress was bringing their order to the table.

Davey was sitting in his room alone when Maggie walked in at the end of the day, having already dismissed the baby-sitter and put a pan of leftover fried chicken in the oven to warm.

"Can we talk?" she said.

He looked at her through sad eyes. "I already know what this is going to be about."

Maggie sat on the edge of the bed. "Yeah?"

"It's about me going to live with Dad. He doesn't want me with him, does he?"

Maggie couldn't have been more surprised. "What makes you say that?"

The boy gave her a snort of disgust. "You should have seen the look on his face when I asked him. It's the same look Molly gives you when you make her eat peas."

Maggie laughed softly and put her arm around the boy. He buried his face against her breast.

"Don't be too disappointed in your father," she said gently. "He loves you very much." She couldn't believe she was saying such nice things about her ex-husband when she'd spent a good half hour on the telephone that afternoon telling her attorney how rotten he was. She was finally prepared to go to court if that's what she had to do. That was the only way she was going to get Bob Farnsworth to take responsibility for his children. At thirty-five, the man had an awful lot of growing up to do. She was thankful that Jason was nothing like him. Instinct told her that Jason Profitt would never turn his back on his responsibility.

"Daddy doesn't want me, does he?" Davey asked, looking up at her through baleful eyes.

She shook her head. "That's not true, son. He doesn't think you'd be happy living with him." She paused. "And he knows how miserable I'd be if you left." Her eyes teared. "Davey, you're the only son I have. I don't want you to go. Your sisters and I love you very much. I'm sorry if I haven't told you enough. I'm sorry if you feel lost in the crowd around here. I will try to spend more time with you in the future."

"I know it's hard," he mumbled. "There's so many of us."

"That doesn't matter," she said. "I wanted every last one of you. I'll try harder to be there for you, Davey. I promise."

"What about Jason?"

"You tell me."

"I don't want to be selfish like Dad. I'm sorry I got mad with you for seeing him. I was just jealous because—" He paused. "I wanted him to like me."

It was difficult to remember her son was only

nine years old sometimes. "He does like you, Davey. Very, very much."

"I'm scared I won't be a good goalie."

"You'll be a wonderful goalie if you want it badly enough."

"Is that all it takes?" he asked hopefully. "Because I really *do* want it."

"That and practice. You still have to work at it." When he nodded, she went on. "Does this mean you're going to be there for the game tonight?" she asked hopefully.

"If Jason will let me. But I don't want you to say anything to him," he added quickly. "I want to talk to him myself."

"I'll make a deal with you," she said. "Suppose I stay out of it altogether and let you two men handle it?" She winked.

"Okay, deal." He shook the hand she offered. "And I don't care if you want to see him as long as you don't act mushy in front of my teammates."

She nodded. "I love you, Davey."

He leaned against her. "I love you too, Mom. Only, don't let the girls know I said that, okay?"

Jason was parked beside Maggie's car when she came out of her office the following Friday. "Hop in," he said, opening the door for her. "We're going for a ride."

"What about my car?"

"It'll be okay. Hurry up, you're blocking traffic." As if to back up his claim, a horn honked from behind.

Laughing to herself, Maggie climbed in beside him. "I appreciate the lift home, Jason, but you realize you'll have to bring me back for my car later."

He grinned. "Don't sweat the small stuff, kid."

Maggie leaned back in the seat and looked at him. He was dressed in neat slacks and a light blue oxford shirt. Both his jacket and tie were draped over the back of the seat. He'd obviously just gotten off work himself. She watched him pull out of the parking lot, then frowned when he drove in the opposite direction from her house. "You're going the wrong way," she said.

"Uh-huh. I'm kidnapping you."

"Very funny. You realize, of course, that I have five children waiting for me at home, not to mention a baby-sitter who gets rather irritable when I'm late, especially on Friday, a date night. I suggest you turn around now before we both end up in trouble."

"Your sitter has already been taken care of, Maggie darlin'. Do you think I would kidnap you without thinking of all these things first?"

"Then who, pray tell, is watching my children?"

"Cynthia and Bob."

"Cynthia and Bob who?"

He grinned. "Your ex-husband Bob, that's who."

At first she was stunned. "How did you get him to agree to that, for heaven's sake?"

"I convinced him you needed the time away. He was *more* than agreeable." Another grin. "Why didn't you tell me you were planning to take him back to court? I think you scared the daylights out of him, 'cause he's doing everything possible to accommodate us."

Maggie pressed her lips into a grim line. "I should have done it a long time ago. Why are we turning onto the interstate, Jason? I never go this way. Where *are* you taking me?"

"The mountains."

"The mountains? That's at least three hours away!"

"Exactly. Why don't you take a little nap. We'll be there before you know it."

"I can't go to the mountains! Anyway, it'll be dark before we get there, and we'll just have to turn around and come back."

"We're not coming back, darlin'." He chuckled at the shocked look she gave him. "At least not tonight. We're staying the weekend."

Maggie was certain she had misunderstood. "The weekend! Have you lost your mind? I don't even have a change of clothes with me."

He winked. "Honey, you won't need clothes where we're going."

It was almost nine o'clock when Jason pulled in in front of an impressive building made entirely of stone. Maggie opened her eyes as soon as he cut the engine. The next thing she knew, a uniformed man was helping her out of the car.

"Welcome to Graystone, ma'am," he said.

"Thank you," she mumbled, still half asleep. Although she had argued and pleaded with Jason for the first hour of the drive, she'd realized she wasn't getting anywhere. Finally, she'd fallen asleep. Anybody who knew Maggie Farnsworth well knew she couldn't ride in a car more than an hour without dozing. Now she was wide awake and more than a little irritated with Jason for whisking her away without warning. "Could you please call me a taxi," she asked the bell captain. "I need to go to the bus station."

Jason chuckled as he rounded the car and put his arms around Maggie. "She's kidding," he told the surprised man. "You know what it's like to try to get a mother to leave her ducklings at home." The man chuckled and moved to the trunk for their bags.

"What are you doing with my suitcase?" Maggie asked Jason when she spied it next to his.

"I asked Cynthia to pack a few things for you."

"You obviously thought of everything. How long have you been plotting this behind my back?"

"Only a couple of days." He grinned. "But I work fast. Now, smile, or people will think you're not having a good time."

Maggie continued to look at him as though she were one breath away from boxing his ears. She followed him and the bell captain into a lobby, where gaily dressed men and women talked among themselves, sitting on comfortable-looking leather couches. On either side of the lobby, or hall, as it was referred to, were massive wood-burning fireplaces complete with roaring fires. Still unable to believe Jason had plotted all this behind her back, Maggie waited for him to check in, then followed the men to an old-fashioned elevator that rattled all the way up to their floor.

Their room was painted a soothing mint green with cream-colored drapes and bedspread. Jason waited until the bell captain had set their bags down, then tipped him and waited for him to leave. "What do you think?"

Maggie honestly didn't know *what* to think. If someone had told her she would be spending the evening in a posh resort hotel with a devastatingly handsome man, she would have told them to take two aspirins and call her back when they felt better. "It's very nice," she said after a moment. "Now, I'd like to call home if you don't mind."

"There's the phone. Why don't you go ahead and check on everybody while I run down to the

THE INCREDIBLE HUNK • 143

restaurant and see if we can get a table. And smile, Maggie." He left her then.

Maggie was both surprised and relieved that all her children were in one piece when she called. "Relax," Cynthia said from the other end. "Everybody is fine. Bob has been in the backyard with Davey all afternoon practicing soccer, if you can believe it. Of course he's done nothing but whine to me that you're taking him back to court. I'm supposed to try to convince you he's a changed man."

The last thing Maggie wanted to discuss at the moment was her ex-husband. But she certainly wasn't going to ask her attorney to back off until Bob proved himself a responsible adult once and for all. "Look, I'm really sorry Jason railroaded you into giving up your weekend to stay with my children. I had no idea—"

Cynthia laughed. "You weren't supposed to know, silly. Now, stop worrying and have a good time. Abby is playing with the girls, and they're all having fun."

Maggie felt better once she had talked to Cynthia and was assured that everything was okay at home. She couldn't help but smile at herself when she thought of all Jason had gone through to surprise her with the weekend. Perhaps she'd been too hard on him. She chuckled as she unzipped the suitcase her friend had secretly packed for her.

"Thank you, Cynthia," Maggie said out loud when she saw the woman had remembered her makeup and toothbrush. Beneath that she found a pair of khaki-colored slacks, a blouse, and the black dress she'd worn on her first date with Jason. The dress had been wrapped in plastic and folded to prevent wrinkling. Maggie shook it out and hung it in the closet next to Jason's garment bag. Finally, there were an old pair of jeans, a sweatshirt, and her comfortable sneakers.

"Looks like you thought of everything, Cynthia." Maggie pulled them out, noticing underneath were her panty hose, a full-length slip, panties, and something else wrapped in tissue paper. She picked up the soft package. Taped on the front was a small card that read: *Have a good time in the mountains. Love, Cynthia.* Smiling, Maggie unwrapped the paper and gasped out loud at the black lace teddy inside. "Oh, Cynthia, what have you done?" She held the flimsy garment up and studied it with a critical eye. It was almost transparent in the light.

Maggie shook her head and stashed the teddy beneath the slip, closed the suitcase, and wondered what on earth she would wear to sleep in. Then, grabbing her makeup and toothbrush, she hurried into the bathroom.

A few seconds later Jason knocked on the bathroom door. "They're holding a table for us downstairs," he said. "Are you ready?"

"I have to run a brush through my hair and put on lipstick," Maggie told him, opening the door. "Am I dressed okay?" The navy split skirt and matching jacket were perfect for work, but she had no idea if it was nice enough for the hotel's dining room.

"You look beautiful, as always." Jason had already slipped on his own jacket. Leaning against the door frame, he watched Maggie apply her lipstick and brush a little blush on her cheekbones. "I like watching you do that," he said when she paused and met his gaze in the mirror. "It's sexy. Later, I plan to lick it off your mouth."

It took every bit of willpower she could muster to

break eye contact with him. Maggie was suddenly all thumbs, trying to fit the tube of lipstick into its sheath and put her things away. Jason stepped closer and put his hands on her shoulder.

"Are you still mad at me?"

She could feel the heat of his touch seeping through the material of her clothes. She tried to look stern, but stern wasn't easy with goose pimples popping out on her neck and shoulders. "No. But the next time you decide to pull something like this, I want to know in advance."

He leaned forward, brushed her hair from the nape of her neck, and pressed his lips there. She shivered. "Are you nervous about spending the weekend with me, Maggie darlin'?"

She smiled shyly. "A little."

"I would never hurt you." When she didn't say anything, he went on. "As much as I enjoyed being with you that first time, Maggie, I did *not* enjoy having you rush out of my bed." He nibbled his way up her neck. "This time when I make love to you, I'm going to be able to hold you all night."

"I'm ready to go," she said a bit breathlessly.

Taking her hand in his, Jason led her out of the room and down the thickly carpeted hallway. They took the elevator to the first floor, where the dining room was located. Maggie was aware that Jason never took his eyes off of her.

"You're making me very self-conscious," she whispered as they waited to be seated.

He looked surprised. "How?"

"By staring at me like that."

"Like what?"

She blushed. "You know perfectly well."

"I like looking at you, Maggie. Is that such a crime?"

She was prevented from answering when the

maître d' appeared and showed them to their table next to a warm fire. "This is lovely," she said to Jason, taking a seat at a table draped in white and bearing a single glass-enclosed candle. "Thank you for bringing me. I'm sorry I gave you such a hard time. It's just—"

Jason took her hand. "What?"

"I feel guilty whenever I leave them."

He knew she was referring to her children. "I know." He squeezed her hand and released it when the waiter appeared with the wine list. Once he'd placed the order, he reclaimed her hand. "So, was everybody doing okay when you called Cynthia?"

Maggie nodded. "She rented several videos. She and Bob plan to take them skating tomorrow. That ought to wear them down." She chuckled. "Not the children. Cynthia and Bob." She sighed. "I'm going to owe her for this one, Jason."

"We both owe her."

"Well, I hope Bob helps out instead of making a nuisance of himself."

"Give him a chance, Maggie. He might surprise us both."

"I hope so. For my children's sake."

"You don't sound very optimistic about that."

"I've known Bob Farnsworth too long. It's not like him to give up an entire weekend."

"Does it bother you having to see him now that you're divorced?"

Maggie was prevented from answering right away when their waiter appeared with their wine. She waited until he poured them each a glass and left. "It bothered me in the beginning," she said. "Even though I knew our marriage was over, it was hard letting go. I was scared."

"Of making it alone?"

She nodded. "It got easier as time went on. I had to forgive him in my heart before I could go on with my life." She chuckled. "Even so, I still get irritated with him when he doesn't take responsibility."

Jason pondered it. "You know, Maggie, I would never run out on you and the kids like that."

Maggie took a sip of her wine. Because she didn't know how to respond to his words, she said nothing.

"You don't believe that, do you?" he asked, giving her a knowing smile.

"All in good time, Jason. All in good time."

Once the waiter returned with menus, Maggie and Jason spent several minutes studying the fare. They ended up ordering an appetizer of marinated artichoke hearts and the filet of sole served with a lemon-butter sauce. Afterward they ordered coffee and shared a slice of pecan pie. Maggie sighed and rubbed her stomach while Jason signed a charge slip. "Have you seen the bell captain?" she asked.

He looked up. "No, why?"

"I think you're going to need help getting me to the room after all that food."

He chuckled softly and helped her out of the chair. Once again they took the old elevator to their room. It wasn't until Jason had closed the door and slid the chain in place that Maggie began to feel nervous again. He shrugged off his jacket, draped it across the back of a chair, and approached her.

"Relax, Maggie."

"I am relaxed."

He chuckled and reached for her. Instead of taking her immediately into his arms, he slowly turned her around and pulled her against him, burying his face in her thick hair. "Your hair smells as if it were washed in sunshine," he said. "Fresh and clean." He raised his hands to it and combed his fingers through the coppery strands. "I need to ask you something."

The way he said it told her it was important. "Yes?"

"That first night together. At my place. I didn't plan it, it just happened. Neither of us took precautions."

He didn't have to spell it out for her. "I can't get pregnant, Jason, if that's what you're asking. I took care of that once Molly was born."

"Took care of it?"

"It's called a tubal ligation. There will be no more babies for me."

Jason was glad she was not looking at him, because he was certain she would read the disappointment in his eyes. "I suppose it's best," he said, thinking of how hectic her life was with five children.

"It seemed so at the time." She turned in his arms, trying to read his face. It was void of emotion. "Uh, Jason . . . I feel rather gritty after working in these clothes all day, not to mention the long drive up."

He smiled. "You want me to run us a bath?"

"Us?" The word came out sounding like a croak in the back of her throat.

"Us." He kissed her lightly on the lips. "Why don't I go ahead and run it," he said, letting her go. "I hope you like it hot."

"Oh, yes, the hotter the better."

Jason hurried into the bathroom and fixed the stopper in place, then turned the water on full blast. "You want me to pour bath gel in?" he called out, peeking around the door.

Maggie, kicking off her low heels, nodded. "Yes, that'll be fine." She picked up her shoes and put them in the closet, then reached for the buttons on her blouse with trembling fingers. This wasn't going to be easy.

"Here, let me do that."

She glanced up in surprise as Jason crossed the room and, with deft fingers, unbuttoned her blouse. Very slowly he slid the garment off her shoulders, then leaned forward and kissed the indentation above her collarbone. Once he helped her out of her split skirt, he draped it over the chair with his jacket and turned toward her, feasting his eyes on her almost-naked body. He reached for the fastening of her bra, but Maggie took a step back.

"I'll do it," she said quickly, blushing as she did so. She didn't want him to see how worn and frayed the elastic was in back.

"No."

Maggie looked up at him, surprised that he was so determined to undress her. If only he would turn out the light, she thought. If only . . .

"Turn around, Maggie."

She did as she was told, her spine growing ramrod-stiff as he fumbled with the hooks. He undid them, then pulled her bra straps down her shoulders and away. Immediately, he moved to her panty hose and underwear.

"Why don't you go ahead and get in the tub, Maggie. Before the water runs over the edge. I'll join you in a second."

Trying to muster up what self-confidence she could find under the circumstances, Maggie made her way into the bathroom, closed the door, and climbed into the tub, shutting the water off as she did so. It wasn't until she was sitting beneath the frothy bubbles that she allowed herself to take a breath of relief.

As Jason sat on the edge of the bed and removed his shoes, he thought of what he'd like to do to Bob Farnsworth. Maggie was so full of insecurities and doubt because of how the man had treated her. No wonder she didn't trust men.

"Never again, Maggie darlin'," he whispered softly. "When you belong to me, you'll never have to worry again." He shucked the rest of his clothes, and, fixing a smile to his face, opened the bathroom door.

At first Maggie was too stunned to do anything more than stare at the man before her. He was magnificent.

"Like what you see, Maggie?" He was smiling.

Maggie glanced away quickly as a bright red blush climbed her neck and splashed across her cheeks. "Jason, I—"

"No need to explain." He chuckled softly as he closed the distance between them. "I like you to look at me. And you're going to see a lot more of me before this weekend is over. Now, scoot that adorable fanny of yours aside so I can get in."

Maggie huddled with her knees against her breasts as Jason climbed into the water, making a lot of noise about how hot it was. Once he was all the way in, he grinned and reached for her.

"Come here, woman."

Maggie went to him shyly. But when their lips made contact, she forgot about everything else, including her sense of modesty. By the time Jason had finished kissing her, their legs were entwined and their wet bodies pressed against each other as though they couldn't get close enough. Jason fumbled for the bar of soap and began to wash her. "You like that, Maggie darlin'?" She nodded, and he laughed softly and kissed her, transferring the soap from his hand to hers. "Now it's your turn to wash me."

Maggie took the bar of soap in both hands and worked up a generous lather, then spread it across his chest and stomach, noting with appreciation the hard lines and taut muscles covered with blond hair. Finally, she lowered her hand between his thighs.

Jason sucked his breath in sharply as her fist closed around him. "Oh, Maggie, you do the nicest things," he said, his lips turning up at the edges. He gazed into her green eyes as she began to stroke him slowly, tenderly, her expression thoughtful. He kissed her hungrily, spearing his tongue deeply into her mouth, past lips and teeth to where it was damp and warm and sweet. All the while she explored him with tentative fingers, stroking him to hardness. When he knew he could take no more, he stilled her eager hands and reached for a towel.

"We're outta here, kid," he said, his voice suddenly husky. He helped her out of the tub, dried her quickly, then led her into the bedroom.

The sheets were clean and fresh and cool against her body as Maggie climbed beneath the bedspread. She dragged it up to her chin, only to have a grinning Jason pull it away. "No secrets tonight, Maggie. I want to look at you."

The light from the bathroom spilled onto the bed and across their bodies as Jason held Maggie in his arms and kissed her. He ran one hand down the small of her back and cupped one round hip, squeezing it until Maggie arched against him. He continued kissing her even as his hand explored between her thighs and dipped inside, where it was warm and wet. "Hmmm, just how I like it," he whispered against her lips. And when Maggie thought he would take her, he drove her to higher heights with his mouth, flicking his tongue across the sensitive bud that housed her desires. Maggie cried out when it got to be too much for her. Only when the sensations began to ebb did Jason enter her and let himself get caught up in the erotic dance. He shuddered in her arms, only a heartbeat after Maggie had climaxed for the second time. And then they collapsed against each other.

"I love you, Maggie," he whispered before he closed his eyes.

Maggie felt as though she'd been given wings.

Ten

At dawn Maggie slipped from the bed, naked and shivering, and made her way into the bathroom, leaving Jason asleep. She came out a few minutes later with a bath towel wrapped around her. Quietly, she tiptoed across the room and peeked between the drapes. She almost gasped aloud at the view outside her window. Mountains. Majestic and awe-inspiring. For as far as the eye could see.

It had been dark when they'd arrived the night before, and Maggie had missed the view that Jason had described as breathtaking. Looking across the valley that made up the small town, her gaze was fixed on the purplish mountain range beyond that seemed to reach into the heavens. Behind them the sun was beginning to rise, casting a golden halo across the mountaintops, making them appear ethereal.

"It's beautiful, isn't it?"

Maggie jumped at the sound of his voice. She had been so taken with the view outside their window, she hadn't heard him get up. Standing behind her, Jason slipped his arms around her waist and pulled her close. She welcomed it, the feel of his hair-rough body, the smell of male flesh, still warm from sleep. She turned in his arms and buried her face against his solid chest. For a moment they merely stood there, bodies flush, her soft curves complementing the hard lines of his body. Finally, Jason tilted her head back for a kiss, and Maggie was certain she had died in the night and gone straight to heaven. He touched her face with his hands and stroked her cheeks with a featherlike caress, then outlined her full mouth. He plowed those same fingers through her hair, grasping her skull tightly, holding her fast while he made love to her waiting mouth. He dragged his lips back and forth across her own with pains-taking slowness, pausing now and then to nibble her trembling bottom lip.

"Why are you wearing this towel?" he whispered when he broke the kiss. Without waiting for an answer he reached for the corner that had been tucked above one breast and pulled it free. The towel fell to her feet softly. Releasing her for a moment, Jason walked to the drapes, tugged the nylon cord, and they whispered open, casting the early morning light into the room. Slipping behind her once again, Jason circled her waist with his arms, and they gazed at the mountains in silence. From time to time he kissed the nape of her neck, toyed with her breasts, and Maggie could sense his desire mounting.

Finally, Jason led her to the bed. "I want you to make love to me," he whispered. "I want you to take control. Do with me as you wish."

The earnest look on his face told her he was serious. "Why?"

"Because I want you to know I'm yours for the

asking. I'm giving myself to you, Maggie, heart and soul."

"I don't know, Jason. I've never—"

"Never what, Maggie? Never taken what you wanted? Never made demands on another human being? Take what you wish from me, sweetheart. It was yours from the beginning." He tilted her face so that she was forced to meet his gaze. "Make love to me, Maggie. Let yourself go. It's safe."

His eyes, brilliantly blue, were filled with such love and yearning, they took her breath away. She shook her head, feeling shy again. "Jason, I don't even know how to begin."

"Start at the beginning. Kiss me."

She sighed. That did not seem so difficult. Rising up on her knees, she leaned over him and touched his lips to hers. He did not respond. She blinked in question.

"*You* kiss *me*," he said.

Maggie kissed him again, this time more fully. He parted his lips, and she slipped her tongue into his mouth. After a while it seemed only natural. She explored him thoroughly. She skimmed his teeth, nibbled at his bottom lip, then sent her tongue deeply into his mouth once more.

While he lay perfectly still, Maggie kissed his eyelids, his temples, his throat, then traced the shell of his ear with her tongue. He shivered. There was power in that, she realized, knowing she could coax such a response from him. She toyed with the crisp curls on his chest, then buried her face against them, brushing her nose back and forth as the golden-brown hair tickled and delighted. His nipples puckered as she teased them with her tongue. She closed her palm around him and began a sensual massage. And finally, because she could stand it no more, she closed her mouth around him and tasted his essence.

Everything else was forgotten as Maggie mounted Jason and made love to him as she had never made love to a man before. In daylight. With the sun spilling in through the windows.

Her body formed a perfect sheath, gripping him tightly. He filled her, and she rode that fullness, and thought she had never seen anything more beautiful than the joining of their bodies. They truly were one; the same as if they shared a single heartbeat. Maggie looked into Jason's eyes and, for a moment, it was as though she were looking into her own soul.

"I love you," she said.

It was her last coherent thought.

She collapsed against him, her coppery hair falling across his chest.

It was sometime later before Maggie had regained her strength. Sprawled across Jason with her face buried against his neck, his hands raised on her fanny, Maggie pushed herself up into a sitting position. She offered Jason a shy grin. "How was I?"

Jason thought she had never looked more beautiful. "You were magnificent."

She sighed happily, stretched out beside him, and snuggled once more against his chest as he covered them with the bedspread. She drifted off to sleep, filled with love for the man beside her.

Later they showered together, taking delight in washing each other, then dressed and went down for a late breakfast. They walked down the narrow mountain road to where the small town lay nestled in the foothills. Holding hands, they visited the shops and art galleries, then stopped off for a cup of hot chocolate.

"I could get used to this," Maggie said, feeling more alive than she had in years.

Jason gazed at her, thinking he had never seen her looking lovelier than she did at that moment, tucked inside a thick sweater. "I love you, Maggie Farnsworth." He leaned forward and touched her nose with his. "Let's go back to the room and take a nap."

"I never take naps."

"Neither do I. Come on."

Back in the room, Maggie felt brave and slipped into the teddy Cynthia had packed for her.

"You're taking a chance wearing that in front of me," Jason said, his eyes devouring her. They made love again, they held each other for a long time. "I'd like to bring you back here at Thanksgiving," Jason said, holding her against his chest. "I understand they go all out decorating for the holidays."

"Hmmm." Maggie had never felt more peaceful.

"We could do some Christmas shopping while we were here."

Maggie laughed softly to herself. "I seriously doubt Cynthia is going to be ready to baby-sit again in less than two weeks. Besides, I can't exclude my children every time you and I want to spend some time together."

"I'm not asking you to, Maggie. But I think you and I deserve some private time."

She sighed. "You know as well as I do it's not easy finding that kind of time." She yawned. "Which reminds me, I need to call home."

Jason raised up. "And I need to go down to the gift shop and buy the troops some souvenirs."

"You don't have to do that."

He shrugged and reached for his clothes. "I want to. It's the least I can do since I stole their mother for the weekend. I'll make dinner reservations while I'm out." He grinned, leaned over, and kissed her on her bare shoulder. "Do *not* put your clothes on while I'm gone."

"You Boy Scouts are all the same. You sway poor, unsuspecting females with those innocent-looking faces, then lure them down the path of ruin."

"But look on the bright side. When you're old and gray, I'll still be around to help you across the street."

It was a nice thought. At the same time, it frightened her.

Maggie waited until she was alone before she called home. "How are you holding out?" she asked Cynthia.

Cynthia laughed. "Well, I took them skating, and I must say it was an experience I won't ever forget."

"What do you mean, *you* took them? Didn't Bob go with you?"

"No. His girlfriend called him last night. Evidently they had a fight, which is the only reason he was here to begin with. Anyway, she was ready to make up, so he left."

"You mean he just stuck you with six children by yourself?" Maggie was furious at the thought.

"It's not as bad as it sounds, Maggie. Actually, the kids have been pretty good. We're going to make cookies this afternoon. Of course, I must warn you the house has been trashed."

She didn't miss the weariness in her friend's

voice. "I'm sorry, Cynthia. I'm going to tell Jason we can't stay a second night."

"Don't be silly. I want you to stay. It's not every day my best friend gets engaged."

"What did you say?"

There was silence on the other end. "Oh, hell," Cynthia muttered. "He hasn't asked you yet, has he?"

"Cynthia, what are you talking about?"

"Maggie, I'm sorry I ruined the surprise. Jason was supposed to pop the question over dinner last night. I figured that's why you were calling me, to give me the good news."

"Pop the question?" Maggie felt the room spin around her.

"Propose, silly. Why do you think Jason went to all the trouble to kidnap you and take you to a romantic inn in the mountains?"

Maggie's head was spinning. "Are you sure about this, Cynthia?"

"I personally helped him select the ring, Maggie." She paused. "I'm so sorry I blew the surprise. Please don't tell Jason I said anything. He'll kill me!"

"He's going to propose marriage?" Maggie said, still filled with shock and disbelief. "But I . . . I mean, we haven't really known each other long. Not even two months yet."

"Maggie, it's obvious the two of you are in love. What else is there to know? And Jason is crazy about your kids. You don't find many men like that, kiddo."

"This is happening too fast. I'm not ready. I don't know *when* I'll be ready."

"Listen, Maggie, don't you *dare* let that man get away," Cynthia warned. "You know what your problem is? You're scared that every man in the world is a jerk like Bob. Well, you're wrong. Bob is a class-A jerk and nobody is ever going to come *close* to him."

"You're right, Cynthia, I *am* scared. I mean, what do I really know about Jason?"

"You know you're in love with him. You know he's a good man. That should be enough."

Maggie was about to answer, when she heard Jason's key in the lock. "Listen, Cynthia, I'll have to call you back. I'm really sorry that you're alone with the children. Let me talk to Jason and get back with you."

"Just don't say anything about you-know-what," her friend told her. "Jason would never forgive me."

"I promise." Maggie barely got the word out of her mouth before Jason came into the room with a shopping bag. She hung up.

"What do you promise?" he said, setting the shopping bag in a chair.

"Huh?" Maggie fidgeted with her hands. "Oh, Cynthia made me promise to stop worrying."

"Stop worrying about the kids, you mean?"

"Bob ran off to be with his girlfriend last night and left Cynthia alone with them."

Jason muttered a curse under his breath. "Looks like I better go back to the gift shop and buy something extra nice for Cynthia, huh?"

"I think I should go home."

"Go home! But I reserved the room for two nights. I just got through making dinner reservations. We can't go home now, Maggie." He sat down beside her on the bed, the expression on his fact hurt. "Besides, I have something special planned for us later."

She knew exactly what that something special was. And it scared the daylights out of her. She needed time. Time to think. Time away from Jason, because it was impossible to think when he was around. "It's not fair dumping the kids on her like this. I won't be able to relax and enjoy myself." She sighed. The more she thought about it, the angrier she got. "If only Bob would come through for me once. I should have known better than to count on him."

"So you're going to punish me for what he did, right?"

"I'm not trying to *punish* anyone. But what you don't seem to understand is the fact that my children come first. I'm sorry, but that's the way it is. You've known from the beginning."

"Listen, Maggie—" Jason paused and took her hand. "I know how important your children are. I've never tried to pretend they weren't. But you can't stop living because you're a mother with responsibilities, and you can't carry around this chip on your shoulder because their father is a louse."

"You think I have a chip on my shoulder?"

"Where men are concerned, yes. I can't help but wonder what that sort of attitude is going to do to your poor son. It's obvious the boy has problems."

Maggie bolted from the bed, dragging the covers with her. "How dare you blame me for Davey's problems," she said. "It never occurred to you to blame his father? Boy, you men really stick together, don't you?"

"If he was so rotten, why'd you stay married for so long? Why did you have five children with him?"

"Because I kept hoping, sooner or later, he'd grow up. But he never did." Suddenly, she realized she was shouting. "He told me he wanted a big family, so I gave it to him, and then he walked out on me."

"You know what I think, Maggie. I think you're the one who wanted the big family. You knew from the beginning how irresponsible Bob was. You were afraid he was going to leave you the way your father did. So you surrounded yourself with children, either because you thought they would *force* him to stay—"

"You don't know what you're talking about! Bob wanted me to abort Molly. He left because I refused." At his look of surprise, she went on. "That's right, I couldn't go through with it. So he walked out on us." Her voice suddenly took on a bitter edge. "Oh, he was real noble about hanging around until I had her and got on my feet again. But you can imagine what it was like all those months living under the same roof with him, me growing bigger every day, not knowing how I was going to work and care for them at the same time." Maggie had to stop to catch her breath. "But you wouldn't know what that's like, would you? You and your hifalutin apartment and sports car. You and your boarding schools and fancy engineering college. You and your West Palm Beach upbringing!"

Maggie was crying now. She was so mad at Bob, she could have scratched his eyes out. Wasn't it just like him to dump his responsibilities in somebody else's lap? And now Jason was telling her to do the same thing. "I can't drop everything every time you want to spend some time alone with me. I have responsibilities. I have obligations. I have five children!" Now she was sobbing. Why would he even think of proposing when they didn't see eye to eye on something as basic as that. Was he out of his mind? "I want to go home, Jason," she said at last. "If you won't take me, then I'll find my own way back."

Jason could stand no more. "Get dressed, Maggie. We're checking out."

Eleven

They made the three-and-a-half-hour drive home in silence. It was the longest ride of Maggie's life. Although she had calmed down somewhat after her outburst, Jason obviously had not. His face looked hard enough to crack. She waited until he pulled into her driveway before saying anything.

"I'm sorry I lost my temper back there," she said. "But you of all people should understand—"

"Oh, I understand all right," he muttered, barely able to contain his frustration. "Ever since I laid eyes on you I've been juggling my life to coincide with yours. Just this once I wanted to spend some time alone with you. Without the children and the ten million other things you have to do." He sighed and raked his hand through his hair. "I didn't even mind the fact that I couldn't come first in your life, Maggie, but I'll be damned if I'm going to settle for always being last. I've tried to understand, really I have. But you're no closer to trusting me or committing yourself to me than the day I met you."

Maggie sat there as tears gathered behind her

eyelids. "What are you saying, Jason?" But she knew darn well what he was saying. He was finished with her. That's the way it always was with men. They could leave if it got to be too much for them. She couldn't. She wouldn't.

He looked at her, and his eyes had lost all their warmth. It was hard for Maggie to believe they'd ever been tender and loving. This was the side of Jason Profitt she had never seen. "From now on, *I* take priority in your life if you want to be with me." He turned the car off long enough to retrieve her suitcase from the trunk. "You know where to find me when you're ready to meet my terms."

"Are you sure you want to go through the trouble of cooking Thanksgiving dinner this year?" Cynthia asked as she and Maggie studied the frozen birds at the grocery store two days before Thanksgiving. "Why don't we split the cost of one of those precooked honey-glazed hams?"

"Hmmm."

"We could make a sweet potato casserole and a green bean casserole and be done with it. What do you think?"

"Hmmm."

"Maggie, are you listening to me?" Cynthia nudged her friend, who was staring off into space.

Maggie jumped. "What did you say?"

"I said it looks like I'm going to have to plan Thanksgiving dinner alone this year. And that's not fair, because if it were up to me, we'd go out to eat instead of spending the day in the kitchen. I do this only because you have to go all out with every holiday, including Groundhog Day. Are you crying again, for Pete's sake!"

"I'm sorry." Maggie realized suddenly her eyes

were watering. "I get weepy every time they play that song about chestnuts roasting on an open fire. Don't you think it's rather early for the stores to be playing Christmas music? We haven't even gotten through Thanksgiving yet." She laughed self-consciously. "I guess I'm not much in the holiday spirit, huh?"

Cynthia frowned. "Gee, what was your first clue, Maggie?" She sighed. "Look, if you don't want to go through this—"

"No, no, the kids deserve a nice meal on Thanksgiving. Let's just hurry up. I'm kind of tired."

"You've *been* tired for almost two weeks now. Ever since you and Jason—"

"I'm fighting a cold," she interrupted. "This has nothing to do with Jason."

"Hrump! You're fighting the lovesick blues, kiddo. Otherwise, you wouldn't have insisted Bob take Davey to soccer."

"It's normal to be depressed during the holidays. At least that's what all the experts say."

"You're not depressed. You have a broken heart."

"My heart is *not* broken." It was a bold-faced lie. She was lower than a mole.

Cynthia pursed her lips. "If your heart were any more broken, we'd have to get a shovel in here to scoop up all the pieces. Why don't you stop pussy-footin' around and call him?"

"Because nothing has changed." Maggie opened the door to the freezer and grabbed a bird and dropped it into the cart. "Okay, we've got that taken care of, now what?"

"You just chose a goose, Maggie. Neither of us has the foggiest idea how to prepare it. Here, let me pick out the turkey this year." She returned the goose to the freezer and chose the biggest turkey she could find. "You know what your problem is, you just don't know when you've got it good."

"Cynthia, you know I love you like a sister, but do me a favor and shut up."

It was hard to believe it was Thanksgiving when the weather in West Palm Beach was in the low sixties, and the fish were biting. Jason studied the cooler filled with mackerel and decided they had caught enough to feed half the town. "We did good, Dad."

Jared Profitt grinned up at his son as he reached into a smaller ice chest and brought out a cold beer. "Darn right we did, boy. This ought to keep your mother in fish for the next six months."

Jason arched one dark brow. "You're not really taking them to her?" He couldn't imagine walking into her spic-and-span kitchen with a bunch of smelly fish.

"Just kidding." The gray-haired man adjusted the cap on his head and chuckled. "You know your mother can't tolerate the smell of fish unless it's served on bone china in a fancy restaurant with lemon on the side. She won't even talk to me till I get the smell scrubbed off my hands. I'll give them away when we reach the pier. You ready to head back?"

Jason popped the top on a cold beer and nodded, thinking about the petite woman in her Christian Dior suits who saw to it her house looked like something out of *Southern Living*. She had been that way for as long as he remembered. Finicky, in a peculiar sort of way. Washing her hands three, four, five times an hour because she was obsessed with keeping herself and the place she lived free of germs. Nothing had changed. Though his father no longer worked sixty to eighty hours per week, he managed to spend enough time on his boat, even sleeping on it at times, so that he did not have to deal with his wife's idiosyncrasies. "Yeah, Mom'll be waiting dinner for us," Jason said after a moment, thinking of the goose she always cooked that he'd never liked. A turkey was too simple, too unsophisticated for her palate. And, of course, they'd have to dress for dinner: coat, tie, the works. "We'd best get back."

The older man started the engine and nudged the throttle gently, and the big boat lifted its bow proudly on the water and made for shore. "Ain't she a beauty, son?"

"She sure is. Does Mom ever come out here with you?"

"Naw. She's too busy with her lunches." He winked. "Besides, she says it messes up her hair."

Both father and son rode the rest of the way in silence, each caught up in his own thoughts. Once back at the pier, they secured the boat, cleaned it up, and found someone who was more than happy to take the fish off their hands. The condo was within walking distance, a stark white building against a backdrop of water and blue sky, overlooking a championship golf course. They were only halfway there when Jared Profitt turned to his son.

"You gonna tell me what's bothering you, or do you plan to keep it to yourself?"

Jason looked up in surprise. "Is it that noticeable?"

"Your mother thinks you've come down with a terminal illness and you're afraid to tell us. She plans to have her doctor examine you before you go home."

"I'm fine, Dad, really."

"Trouble with your new job?" When Jason shook his head, his father went on. "Is it a woman?"

Jason chuckled and regarded the man who had never had much time for him growing up. Now he had more than enough time on his hands, but Jason lived too far away to visit often. "Yeah, it's a woman."

"I figured as much." He paused and brought out a pack of cigarettes. "Want one?"

Jason shook his head. "I thought you gave that up a long time ago."

"I get the urge every once in a while. Don't tell your mother." He paused and sat on a bench shaded by palm trees. The whole area was green and lush and perfectly manicured. It reeked of money. "So what's the problem? I mean, there's got to be a reason why you're walking around sour-faced."

"She has five children."

"Jeez!"

"It's not a problem for me. It's her." Jason sat down next to his father and tried to explain. He told him about the hard time Maggie had, her irresponsible ex-husband, the overwhelming responsibilities, everything. Even the diamond engagement ring he'd purchased that was sitting in his top dresser drawer.

"But son, five kids!"

"I know, Dad. And I was scared at first, believe me. But I'm crazy about her kids. I know I could do right by them. I would never have bought that engagement ring had I not thought it through carefully. And I wasn't going to press her into getting married right away. I would've given her all the time she needed. I just wanted her to know it was for keeps. That I would be around for as long as she wanted me."

"So what happened?"

"She won't commit. She thinks all men are bastards because she's had a bad experience with one." He shook his head sadly. "I've tried to be patient and understanding." Suddenly, he looked almost boyish. "You'd like her, Dad. She's convinced her hectic life would drive the Pope to swearing, but her house is so full of love and laughter." Jason gazed across the water as he spoke, watching the sea gulls hunt for their afternoon meal. He thought of the past two weeks without Maggie. He'd missed her something fierce. He missed seeing her at the soccer games, cheering them on, missed getting together with her and her brood afterward, missed those long, intimate telephone conversations they often had once the kids were in bed. He missed holding her, loving her. The joy had simply gone out of his life. The only contact he had with her these days was being near her son. Gazing into Davey's green eyes and watching the breeze play in his coppery hair, he saw Maggie all over again and was reminded of his loss.

"What are you going to do?" Jared asked after a moment.

"I told her if she wanted me, she could pick up the phone and call, but she's so stubborn, she won't even think of doing something like that. It's over."

"I wish I could help you, son. There isn't anything I wouldn't do to help."

They made their way back to the condo. Jason dreaded going back inside the posh living quarters with the pristine white carpet and dainty teal sofas that looked as if they belonged in a dollhouse or a showroom window. His mother would have pulled off the protective covers for the holiday. He longed for Maggie's place with its clutter and toys and laughter, where the furniture was never draped in sheets, where you weren't expected to take your shoes off every time you came in the house, where stray animals were welcome and every kid in the neighborhood felt at home.

"Don't give up on what you want, Jason," Jared Profitt said as they neared the ocean-front building. "One day you'll be an old man like me, and it'll be too late to start over."

And then Jason understood why his father had preferred work to coming home. It hadn't been because of him. It felt good knowing that. At the same time, it was sad.

"Davey, grab me that box of tissues," Maggie said a split second before she let out a loud, unladylike sneeze that all but knocked the magazine she'd been reading off her lap.

"Good grief, Mom!" Davey, sitting at the foot of the bed, watching cartoons on a small black-and-white portable, jumped out of the way. "You're spreading germs like crazy, you know."

"Don't tell me your problems," she muttered. "You're the one who gave me this cold in the first place. Where's Jessie?"

"She's in the kitchen, making lunch. She and the twins refuse to come in here while we're sick. Aunt Cynthia says she won't even drive her car down our street for fear of catching something."

"Smart girls." Maggie leaned back against her pillow and sighed. The cold she'd been fighting had turned into the flu the day before. She'd come home from work ready to crawl under the covers and die, only to discover Davey and Molly had been stricken as well. She glanced down at her youngest, who was sleeping beside her. Although her fever had subsided, thanks to the medicine, Maggie knew it would be several days before the girl was back to normal. By then the twins would have it. She blew her nose. "I hate this," she muttered. "I'm never sick."

"Aunt Cynthia says it's because you have a broken heart."

"Aunt Cynthia has been reading too many romance novels."

"Why don't you call him, Mom?"

"Him?"

"You know who I'm talking about. Jason. I know you don't like me to talk about him, but I can't pretend he doesn't exist. Who are you going to get to help you now that Dad is marrying that bimbo and moving to Texas?"

The bimbo, of course, was the word they all used to refer to the woman in Bob's life. The kids had started saying it when they'd heard her use the word talking to Cynthia. She felt bad. "You shouldn't say that about your father's fiancée," she admonished her son gently. "And as for what I'll do, I'll do what I've always done. Your father wasn't exactly my Rock of Gibraltar, you know." Frankly, she was glad to see Bob go, and she figured the only reason he was transferring to Texas in the first place was to make it more difficult for her to get money out of him. The crime was the fact that his children would never get to know their father. She had suffered her moments of guilt over that fact, but knowing there wasn't a darn thing she could do about it, she'd tried to get past it. She and her children had one another, that's all that mattered. Even so, she knew they would not always be there.

Jason had accused her of having them to keep Bob from leaving. That wasn't it, she knew. In her heart she knew that her reasons weren't entirely unselfish. She had seen it as a way to keep from being alone again. But somewhere along the way she'd realized that was absolutely no reason to have children. Children were borrowed only for a short time. It was up to her to raise them to be strong, independent creatures, even if it meant they would no longer need her. And in teaching them these things, she'd become strong and independent herself. She'd learned she wasn't weak like her mother, who'd married a man she didn't love so she'd have someone to take care of her. Being alone no longer terrified her.

Maggie realized suddenly that her son was staring at her. "What's wrong? Do I look that bad?"

"I'm worried about you, Mom. You used to smile all the time when Jason was around. Now you mope around like—" He paused. "Like you lost your best friend."

Maggie felt the sting of tears. They were always so close, only a heartbeat away, and they had Jason Profitt's name written all over them. She loved him and couldn't bear the thought of never seeing him again, of not spending the rest of her life with him. Finally, she turned away, not wanting her son to see her cry. But she knew Davey had seen her tears. He stood and made his way to the door. "Where are you going?" Maggie asked.

He paused and gave his mother a baleful look. "To my room."

Only when he was out of sight did Maggie allow the rest of the tears to fall. She grabbed the box of tissues. She had cried enough tears lately to create a fishing hole in the neighborhood. Her and her damn pride! She had picked up the phone several times to call Jason, only to hang up before it had a chance to ring. What would she say to him? Now even more than before she had too many responsibilities.

Exhausted from both her cold and tears, Maggie pulled the covers to her chin and closed her eyes. She had to be well Monday. She had to put everything else out of her mind and concentrate on getting better.

The telephone was ringing when Jason stepped out of the shower. He grabbed a towel, wrapped it haphazardly around his middle, and hurried into the bedroom, snatching it up on the third ring. "Hello?"

"Jason?"

"Davey?" He recognized the boy's voice immediately.

"Yeah, it's me."

Jason smiled into the phone and sat on the edge of the bed. He'd missed the boy. "What's up, kid? You sound different."

"I have a cold. We all do."

"Everybody?"

"Now, just me and Mom and Molly."

"That's too bad."

"Mom never gets sick. Aunt Cynthia says she has a broken heart."

Jason sat very still on the bed. Something inside started to ache at the thought of Maggie, *his* Maggie, suffering in any way. But he tried to make his voice sound light. "No kiddin'?"

"It's because of you, Jason," the boy said. "She misses you."

Jason squeezed his eyes closed, trying to block out the emotions that surged through him. Had a man ever loved a woman as much? he wondered. Finally, he realized Davey was waiting on the other end of the line. "Listen, your mother has my number if she needs me," he said.

"She won't call," the boy said glumly.

"Then there's not much I can do. She knows where to find me. All she has to do is let me know, and I'll be there." He sighed, knowing how desperately Davey needed a man in his life. He would have done well by the boy, by all of them. Being at his parents and seeing what their life was like had reinforced those feelings. But Maggie Farnsworth was convinced she didn't need him or anybody else in her life.

"I'm sorry, Davey. Really sorry." He started to hang up.

"Uh, Jason?"

"Yeah?"

"If you won't come for her, would you do it for me?"

Whispers.

Slipping deeper beneath the warm covers, Maggie tried to ignore them, but they wouldn't go away. She opened her eyes slowly. Jason Profitt was standing beside the bed with a food tray. A dream, no doubt. Too much medicine was making her see things that weren't really there.

"Can you sit up?" he asked softly.

"Jason?" Her voice trembled.

"In the flesh, darlin'. Here, sit up and try to take some soup." Jason nodded to Jessie, who was still standing in the doorway. She pulled the others out of the room, including Molly, and closed the door behind them.

Maggie shifted in the bed, then pushed herself up slowly. "When? How long have you been here?" she asked.

"Not long. Davey called and said he was worried about you. How long have you been sick?" He set the tray on her lap, watching closely that she did not upset it.

"Oh, I've been fighting it for a week, and then it hit me yesterday at work." She offered him a weak smile, wondering how bad she looked in her wrinkled pajamas.

"Why didn't you call me, Maggie?"

It was on the tip of her tongue to tell him how many times she'd picked up the phone to do that very thing. She lowered her gaze. "I didn't think you'd come," she answered truthfully.

Jason gazed back at her for a moment before he took a seat on the edge of the bed. "How could you *possibly* think that, Maggie? When are you ever going to realize how much I love you? As well as your children," he added.

She struggled with her emotions for a moment. She was tempted to tell him Bob was leaving, but she didn't. She didn't want Jason to think she was desperate for a father figure. She didn't want him to feel sorry for her or think she couldn't handle things alone. But she couldn't stop the tears from falling. "I've missed you so," she said, choking on a sob.

He took her hand. "I know, baby. I've missed you too."

She mopped her tears with a tissue. "I didn't think it was possible to miss someone that much. It scares me to want you so badly. I feel—" She paused. "Like I'm out of control."

"There have been times in my life when I was scared to be close to anyone, Maggie. But when I met you—" He paused. "I knew it was right. I knew because I had been searching for you all my life."

Maggie studied him closely, meeting his gaze. It was full of love and acceptance. She took a deep breath. "I'm going to go out on a limb here, Jason," she said, her voice trembling. "I'm going to admit to things I never thought I'd say to another human being." She paused and took another deep breath. "I love you, Jason Profitt, and I need you in my life. Not just today but tomorrow and the next day and—" She laughed self-consciously. "The day after that. There, I said it."

He smiled. "How did it feel?"

"Like a weight has been lifted off my shoulders." Suddenly, she frowned. "But if you ever leave me, Jason, or make me eat those words, I swear I'll hunt you down like the lowest dog and—"

He stopped her with a kiss, and the tray almost slipped off her lap. He caught it. "Does this mean you'll marry me?"

"Yes. And I promise I won't put you last in my life. I'll do my best, Jason."

He pondered it. "Would it bother you to quit your job?"

"Quit my job?"

"And let me take care of you and the kids for a while so we can concentrate on being a family. If your job means a lot to you, you can always go back to it when Molly's older and doesn't need you as much."

To Maggie it sounded like a gift from heaven. She could finally do the things she'd always wanted to do for her children. She would live without all the guilt that working mothers so often had to deal with. "Are you sure you want all that responsibility, Jason?"

He nodded. "I wouldn't be here if I didn't. As much as I love you, it should come as no surprise that I love your children as well. I would gladly adopt them, Maggie."

"What about having a child of your own? You know I can't anymore. I mean, they say tubals are reversible, but—"

"Why don't we take our time and enjoy the children we have. We can talk about this a couple of years from now. I still want us to have our time together. Another reason for wanting you to be a full-time mommy. Because there will be times when I won't want to share you with the children. I'm going to want to take you back up to the mountains and make love to you all weekend."

Her eyes teared. "I don't know what to say. I'm touched. Overwhelmed. You really are a Prince Charming."

"Just say yes, Maggie, and we'll start from there."

"Yes."

He kissed her once again, this time tenderly. "I love you, Maggie. Don't ever forget it."

Jason picked up the spoon and dipped it into the bowl of soup he'd heated for her. "Now, be a good girl and eat something," he said. "I can't very well take you down the aisle until you get your strength back. I hope you won't ask for a long engagement. I'd like to be married by Christmas."

"That sounds perfect." She opened her mouth as Jason fed her several spoonfuls of soup. Finally, she chuckled. "Can you believe this? I mean, all this time I've been stating unequivocally how I *didn't* need a man in my life, and here you are spoon-feeding me? What would people think?"

Jason laughed as well. "I'm just practicing, Maggie darlin', for when you're old and have no teeth, and I have to feed you applesauce and mashed peas."

"You plan to be around that long, huh?"

"You can count on it, babe."

THE EDITOR'S CORNER

Next month LOVESWEPT salutes **MEN IN UNIFORM**, those daring heroes who risk all for life, liberty . . . and the pursuit of women they desire. **MEN IN UNIFORM** are experts at plotting seductive maneuvers, and in six fabulous romances, you'll be at the front lines of passion as each of these men wages a battle for the heart of the woman he loves.

The first of our dashing heroes is Brett Upton in **JUST FRIENDS** by Laura Taylor, LOVESWEPT #600—and he's furious about the attack on Leah Holbrook's life, the attack that cost her her memory and made her forget the love they'd once shared and that he'd betrayed. Now, as he desperately guards her, he dares to believe that fate has given him a second chance to win back the only woman he's ever wanted. Laura will hold you spellbound with this powerful romance.

In **FLYBOY** by Victoria Leigh, LOVESWEPT #601, veteran Air Force pilot Matt Cooper has seen plenty of excitement, but nothing compares to the storm of desire he feels when he rescues Jennifer Delaney from a raging typhoon. Matt has always called the world his home, but the redhead suddenly makes him long to settle down. And with wildfire embraces and whispers of passionate fantasies, he sets out to make the independent beauty share his newfound dream. A splendid love story, told with plenty of Victoria's wit.

Patricia Potter returns to LOVESWEPT with **TROUBA-DOUR,** LOVESWEPT #602. Connor MacLaren is fiercely masculine in a kilt—and from the moment she first lays eyes on him, Leslie Turner feels distinctly overwhelmed. Hired as a publicist for the touring folk-singer, she'd expected anything except this rugged Scot who awakens a reckless hunger she'd never dare confess. But armed with a killer grin and potent kisses, Connor vows to make her surrender to desire. You'll treasure this enchanting romance from Pat.

In her new LOVESWEPT, **HART'S LAW,** #603, Theresa Gladden gives us a sexy sheriff whose smile can melt steel. When Johnny Hart hears that Bailey Asher's coming home, he remembers kissing her breathless the summer she was seventeen—and wonders if she'd still feel so good in his embrace. But Bailey no longer trusts men and she insists on keeping her distance. How Johnny convinces her to open her arms—and heart—to him once more makes for one of Theresa's best LOVESWEPTs.

SURRENDER, BABY, LOVESWEPT #604 by Suzanne Forster, is Geoff Dias's urgent message to Miranda Witherspoon. A soldier of fortune, Geoff has seen and done it all, but nothing burns in his memory more than that one night ten years ago when he'd tasted fierce passion in Miranda's arms. When he agrees to help her find her missing fiancé, he has just one objective in mind: to make her see they're destined only for each other. The way Suzanne writes, the sexual sparks practically leap off the page!

Finally, in **HEALING TOUCH** by Judy Gill, LOVESWEPT #605, army doctor Rob McGee needs a wife to help him raise his young orphaned niece—but what he wants is

Heather Tomasi! He met the lovely temptress only once two years before, but his body still remembers the silk of her skin and the wicked promises in her eyes. She's definitely not marriage material, but Rob has made up his mind. And he'll do anything—even bungee jump—to prove to her that he's the man she needs. Judy will delight you with this wonderful tale.

On sale this month from FANFARE are four fabulous novels. From highly acclaimed author Deborah Smith comes **BLUE WILLOW,** a gloriously heart-stopping love story with characters as passionate and bold as the South that brought them forth. Artemas Colebrook and Lily MacKenzie are bound to each other through the Blue Willow estate . . . and by a passion that could destroy all they have struggled for.

The superstar of the sensual historical, Susan Johnson tempts you with **SINFUL.** Set in the 1780s, Chelsea Ferguson must escape a horrible fate—marriage to a man she doesn't love—by bedding another man. But Sinjin St. John, Duke of Seth, refuses to be her rescuer and Chelsea must resort to a desperate deception that turns into a passionate adventure.

Bestselling LOVESWEPT author Helen Mittermeyer has penned **THE PRINCESS OF THE VEIL,** a breathtakingly romantic tale set in long-ago Scotland and Iceland. When Viking princess Iona is captured by the notorious Scottish chief Magnus Sinclair, she vows never to belong to him, though he would make her his bride.

Theresa Weir, author of the widely praised **FOREVER,** delivers a new novel of passion and drama. In **LAST SUMMER,** movie star Johnnie Irish returns to his Texas hometown, intent on getting revenge. But all thoughts of getting even disappear when he meets the beautiful widow Maggie Mayfield.

Also on sale this month in the hardcover edition from Doubleday is **SACRED LIES** by Dianne Edouard and Sandra Ware. In this sexy contemporary novel, Romany Chase must penetrate the inner sanctum of the Vatican on a dangerous mission . . . and walk a fine line between two men who could be friend or foe.

Happy reading!

With warmest wishes,

Nita Taublib

Nita Taublib
Associate Publisher
LOVESWEPT and FANFARE

OFFICIAL RULES TO WINNERS CLASSIC SWEEPSTAKES

No Purchase necessary. To enter the sweepstakes follow instructions found elsewhere in this offer. You can also enter the sweepstakes by hand printing your name, address, city, state and zip code on a 3" x 5" piece of paper and mailing it to: Winners Classic Sweepstakes, P.O. Box 785, Gibbstown, NJ 08027. Mail each entry separately. Sweepstakes begins 12/1/91. Entries must be received by 6/1/93. Some presentations of this sweepstakes may feature a deadline for the Early Bird prize. If the offer you receive does, then to be eligible for the Early Bird prize your entry must be received according to the Early Bird date specified. Not responsible for lost, late, damaged, misdirected, illegible or postage due mail. Mechanically reproduced entries are not eligible. All entries become property of the sponsor and will not be returned.

Prize Selection/Validations: Winners will be selected in random drawings on or about 7/30/93, by VENTURA ASSOCIATES, INC., an independent judging organization whose decisions are final. Odds of winning are determined by total number of entries received. Circulation of this sweepstakes is estimated not to exceed 200 million. Entrants need not be present to win. All prizes are guaranteed to be awarded and delivered to winners. Winners will be notified by mail and may be required to complete an affidavit of eligibility and release of liability which must be returned within 14 days of date of notification or alternate winners will be selected. Any guest of a trip winner will also be required to execute a release of liability. Any prize notification letter or any prize returned to a participating sponsor, Bantam Doubleday Dell Publishing Group, Inc., its participating divisions or subsidiaries, or VENTURA ASSOCIATES, INC. as undeliverable will be awarded to an alternate winner. Prizes are not transferable. No multiple prize winners except as may be necessary due to unavailability, in which case a prize of equal or greater value will be awarded. Prizes will be awarded approximately 90 days after the drawing. All taxes, automobile license and registration fees, if applicable, are the sole responsibility of the winners. Entry constitutes permission (except where prohibited) to use winners' names and likenesses for publicity purposes without further or other compensation.

Participation: This sweepstakes is open to residents of the United States and Canada, except for the province of Quebec. This sweepstakes is sponsored by Bantam Doubleday Dell Publishing Group, Inc. (BDD), 666 Fifth Avenue, New York, NY 10103. Versions of this sweepstakes with different graphics will be offered in conjunction with various solicitations or promotions by different subsidiaries and divisions of BDD. Employees and their families of BDD, its division, subsidiaries, advertising agencies, and VENTURA ASSOCIATES, INC., are not eligible.

Canadian residents, in order to win, must first correctly answer a time limited arithmetical skill testing question. Void in Quebec and wherever prohibited or restricted by law. Subject to all federal, state, local and provincial laws and regulations.

Prizes: The following values for prizes are determined by the manufacturers' suggested retail prices or by what these items are currently known to be selling for at the time this offer was published. Approximate retail values include handling and delivery of prizes. Estimated maximum retail value of prizes: 1 Grand Prize ($27,500 if merchandise or $25,000 Cash); 1 First Prize ($3,000); 5 Second Prizes ($400 each); 35 Third Prizes ($100 each); 1,000 Fourth Prizes ($9.00 each) ; 1 Early Bird Prize ($5,000); Total approximate maximum retail value is $50,000. Winners will have the option of selecting any prize offered at level won. Automobile winner must have a valid driver's license at the time the car is awarded. Trips are subject to space and departure availability. Certain black-out dates may apply. Travel must be completed within one year from the time the prize is awarded. Minors must be accompanied by an adult. Prizes won by minors will be awarded in the name of parent or legal guardian.

For a list of Major Prize Winners (available after 7/30/93): send a self-addressed, stamped envelope entirely separate from your entry to: Winners Classic Sweepstakes Winners, P.O. Box 825, Gibbstown, NJ 08027. Requests must be received by 6/1/93. DO NOT SEND ANY OTHER CORRESPONDENCE TO THIS P.O. BOX.